A Pity Youth Does Not Last

The Poet

MICHEÁL O'GUIHEEN

A PITY YOUTH
DOES NOT LAST

Reminiscences of the Last of
the Great Blasket Island's
Poets and Storytellers

TRANSLATED FROM THE IRISH
BY TIM ENRIGHT

Oxford New York

OXFORD UNIVERSITY PRESS

Oxford University Press, Walton Street, Oxford OX2 6DP
Oxford New York Toronto
Delhi Bombay Calcutta Madras Karachi
Petaling Jaya Singapore Hong Kong Tokyo
Nairobi Dar es Salaam Cape Town
Melbourne Auckland
and associated companies in
Berlin Ibadan

English translation © Timothy Enright 1982

Irish edition published by Government Publications, Dublin, 1953
Original poetry, under the title Coinnle Corra,
published by An Clóchomhar Teoranta, Dublin, 1968

First issued as an Oxford University Press paperback 1982
Reprinted 1992

All rights reserved. No part of this publication may be reproduced,
stored in a retrieval system, or transmitted, in any form or by any means,
electronic, mechanical, photocopying, recording, or otherwise, without
the prior permission of Oxford University Press

This book is sold subject to the condition that it shall not, by way
of trade or otherwise, be lent, re-sold, hired out or otherwise circulated
without the publisher's prior consent in any form of binding or cover
other than that in which it is published and without a similar condition
including this condition being imposed on the subsequent purchaser

British Library Cataloguing in Publication Data
O'Guiheen, Mícheál
A pity youth does not last.
1. Blasket Islands, Ire.—Social life and customs.
I. Title II. Is truagh na fannan an óige.
English
941.9'6   D990.B6
ISBN 0-19-281320-X

Printed in Great Britain by
Richard Clay Ltd
Bungay, Suffolk

Fate turned against us,
It left me here deserted.

CONTENTS

List of Illustrations

ACKNOWLEDGEMENTS

and a Note on the Translation

I HAVE to thank George Thomson for painstakingly going through the translation and making useful suggestions, as well as writing a Foreword. I have also to thank my wife, Trudy, for her help throughout.

Acknowledgements are due to the Department of Education, Irish Publications Branch, Dublin, for permission to publish this translation of Micheál O'Guiheen's autobiography, and to An Clóchomhar Teoranta, Dublin, for permission to publish this translation of some of the poems.

I also wish to thank Judith Chamberlain and Bob Knowles of Oxford University Press for their meticulous editorial care.

The photos are by courtesy of Frank Lewis and the West Kerry Development Co-operative, Seosamh O'Duiginn and Clódhanna Teoranta, Kevin Danaher and University College, Dublin, Walter McGrath and the 'Cork Examiner', and George Thomson.

The translation is into my own Kerry English, the language Micheál O'Guiheen would have used if Irish had disappeared from the Great Blasket, as it had from my own part of Kerry long before I was born. Here I have followed in the footsteps of my old schoolmaster, Bryan MacMahon, translator of *Peig*.

T. E.

FOREWORD

Micheál O'Guiheen was the last of a long line of poets and storytellers, custodians of a rich popular culture going back to the middle ages and beyond. He learnt the art from his mother, Peig Sayers, whose name is known to all students of Gaelic folklore. Born and bred in the Great Blasket Island, he was a schoolmate of Maurice O'Sullivan, author of *Twenty Years A-Growing*. His brothers and sisters all emigrated to the United States. So, too, did he, but after a few months there he returned, having failed to 'make good'. America offered these exiles an escape from the poverty of their home life, but only on condition that they surrendered their cultural values. Some paid this price without regret, others only with a life-long sense of loss; for a few it was too heavy, and they came home.

When Micheál returned from America, his island community was on the verge of extinction. A few years later, he and his mother, now a widow, moved out to the mainland and settled in the place where she had been born – a little cluster of homesteads in the shadow of Mount Eagle. She died in 1958, and Micheál spent the rest of his life there alone.

I met him on my first visit to the Island in 1923, and we became close friends. He was different from the other boys – studious and introspective. It was his great hope that one day he might 'go to college'. After 1934 I lost touch with him. I met him for the last time in 1966. As I remembered it, the visitor to the little hamlet where he lived had been greeted by the barking of dogs and cockcrows and children's cries; but now there was silence, and the footpath was overgrown. When Micheál opened the door to me, I had to explain who I

was, because he was not expecting me, and he was now nearly blind. He was overjoyed, and we spent an hour together
casting our minds back to the days of our youth, which he
recalled as vividly as if it had all happened only the week
before.

  He published three books – this, a biography of his mother,
and a sheaf of poems. Besides his lost youth, he laments the
lost way of life, which, in common with many of his genera-
tion, he had hoped to see re-created in an Ireland 'united and
Gaelic and free'. His story is very different from Maurice's,
because he lacked Maurice's *joie de vivre*; yet, when it came to
a choice between the old world and the new, they both chose
the old. If Micheál had 'made good' in the new world, he
might have had a happier life, but then this last of the Blasket poets and storytellers would have left no written memo-
rial.

GEORGE THOMSON

Birmingham, 1979

INTRODUCTION

1

'I WROTE this in loving memory of the place where I was born and of the people that I knew,' says Micheál O'Guiheen, "The Poet", of his book. The place was the Great Blasket Island, three miles by one, largest of a cluster of islands off the coast of Kerry in the South-West of Ireland.

These islands were the home of a remarkable community literature arising out of a way of life and a heritage shared by all; a wealth of poetry and story-telling; and everyday speech in which delight was taken in verbal dexterity, the apt *mot* or proverb, timely quotations from verse ancient and modern, humorous parallels between their own daily round and the deeds of heroes in the old sagas.

George Thomson, translator of one of the best known of the Blasket books, Maurice O'Sullivan's *Twenty Years A-Growing*, wrote of this tradition: 'We have a small library the like of which is not to be found in any other language. They are books apart which have won a corner for themselves in international literature.'[1]

Micheál O'Guiheen's book was for the Gaelic-speaking world, but also for the Islanders themselves. Introducing it, he said that he wanted 'to place a small picture before those people that I knew, so that if my work succeeds they will be all the more thankful to me.... I have given an account of the people living on the Island in my time and the kind of life they had, of their grand wise talk about the things that mattered to them.' He held these aims in common with both Maurice O'Sullivan and Tomás O'Crohan, author of *The Islandman* and pioneer of the Blasket writers.

[1] *An Blascaod a Bhí (The Blasket that Was)*, Maynooth 1977.

2

Before the Great Famine of the 1840s there were Gaelic-speakers in every county in Ireland. For Gaelic the Great Death was the Great Silence. Struck down by starvation and disease its life blood flowed away on a swelling tide of emigration until by the end of the century it was clinging mainly to the rim of the western seaboard. The Great Blasket, rich in wild-life and sea food, had been a refuge for those fleeing from evictions on the mainland during the eighteenth and nineteenth centuries. Among those settling there after the Great Famine were the poets Seán O'Donlevy and Micheál O'Sullivan, great-grandfather of Micheál O'Guiheen, "The Poet".

A body to revive Irish, the Gaelic League, was formed in 1893 and it won wide support. Students of the language began to arrive in the Gaeltachts, or Gaelic-speaking areas. The Blasket Islanders were unaware of their great cultural riches until scholars began to cross the three miles of sea to live among them, record their lore and urge them to take to the pen too. Scholars came from the mainland and also from further afield, among them Carl Marstrander the Norwegian in 1907 to be followed by Carl Wilhelm von Sydow from Sweden, Robin Flower, George Thomson, and Kenneth Jackson from England.

A pride in their Gaelic heritage grew among the Islanders along with an awareness, beginning with Tomás O'Crohan, that their way of life was doomed. Micheál O'Guiheen's story is of the Island dying. When his book begins in 1904 the Blasket Islanders numbered about 150 people. They lived mainly by fishing for mackerel. In 1921 there were 400 currachs – canvas covered canoes manned by three or four oarsmen – fishing off the West Kerry coast. By 1934 there were barely 80. An economic whirlwind had struck. Deep-sea trawlers had moved in to scour the sea beds, and the men of the currach could not compete with the giants of capital. In a poem, *One Fine Morning*,[1] Micheál O'Guiheen wrote:

> The mist streamed in ribbons of silk,
> Beyond everything the fish were rising,
> Shoaling on the sea's waters –
> Sharp woe! Where had the boats departed?
>
> The cormorant, black, thin-necked,
> Floated like a bottle on the water,
> White sea-gulls swarmed wildly,
> Tearing the fish, gulping it.

The Great Blasket was doomed. It was the next parish to America and soon Springfield, Massachusetts, to which the young emigrated, became a household name more familiar to the Islanders than Tralee. Swept up too in the nets of the giant trawlers was the most ancient form extant of the Gaelic language and a tradition of poetry and story-telling that had been elaborately woven down the centuries.

Of the change in attitude towards the Irish language Micheál O'Guiheen writes:

It is many the trip I made to Dingle in my young days, and to tell the truth we were little short of preferring to be dead. We were people of no heed at all in Dingle, when we wouldn't have English. But there's a big change over the people of Dingle since then. The small children that are there today have fluent Irish and so have most of the shopkeepers. (p. 118)

---

[1] Translated from the collection of his poems, *Coinnle Corra* – 'Wild Hyacinths' – published by An Clóchomhar Teoranta, Dublin. Ten of these, which seem most apposite to his theme, appear in a literal translation on pp. 125–37 below.

And in a poem, *The False Voice*:

> They think it was not misfortune
> That sent them astray –
> English is their gentility,
> By English they were bereft.

Of course the shopkeepers always had Irish but it was not the language of Church or State, of social advance. I recall a story told to me by Peig Sayers, Micheál's mother and the queen of Gaelic story-telling: Four Islanders, after making money on fish, went to Dingle to buy suits of clothes. They entered a shop and asked for what they wanted in their only language, Irish. The shopkeeper replied in English. 'If that's the case,' said the Islanders, 'we'll go to another shop where we will be understood.' They were making for the door when the shopkeeper rushed after them, spouting Irish.

All this was changed by the scholars making their pilgrimage to the Western Island. The Islanders were proud when the first Blasket books appeared in Irish; prouder still when they appeared in English, translated for a worldwide audience by Robin Flower, Moya Llewelyn Davies, and George Thomson.

3

Micheál O'Guiheen was a poet, and known as "The Poet", in a community where poetry was traditionally held in the highest honour. In earlier centuries the poets were a powerful caste and in the schools of classical Gaelic poetry they received a long and rigorous training in traditional lore as well as versification. These schools disappeared as Elizabethan, Cromwellian, and Williamite plantations followed each other and the Penal Laws were clamped on Gaeldom. The poets were dispersed among the peasantry and a rich seam was added to the mine of folktale and song that had always existed alongside the literary schools. Gaelic poetry with its intricate patterns of external and internal rhymes, assonance and alliteration, is basically aural and the word-music is difficult to reproduce in English without straining the meaning to fit the metre.

Micheál O'Guiheen, the last of the Blasket poets and storytellers, was steeped in the tradition. At one stage in his autobiography he breaks out into poetry to express the depth of his feelings (pp. 88–9), just as the early Irish hero tales were interspersed with lyric verse. The opening poem of his collection of 32, published in 1970, ends:

> By all scripts of seers and druids,
> The most famed in Ireland,
> The tide spreads a mantle of silk
> Around the Blasket Island.

In his poems "The Poet" reveals again and again the exile's heart. He might be in faraway America, though he is actually on the mainland within sight of the Blaskets. Besides local events, which had always inspired poetry and song, his main themes are exile, loneliness, man alienated – the poet's *cri de coeur*.

4

Story-telling was also an ancient craft, its best exponents highly esteemed. Of Micheál O'Guiheen Professor Bo Almqvist writes: 'One can scarcely find it credible that one single man could have possessed such a rich store of oral lore. In the archives of the Department of Irish Folklore there are over 8,400 pages, written by Micheál himself in his characteristic and beautiful hand. Most of this material was taken from Micheál's own memory, although he also collected from his mother – the famous storyteller Peig Sayers – and from another Blasket woman, Máire Ní Shé (Méiní). These collections deal with almost all aspects of folklore: different genres of oral literature, beliefs, customs, and material folk culture.'[1]

It was while listening to stories and songs that the long hours floated away for the Islanders during the dark winter nights. Young and old would flock to the gathering-house. First the fiddler tuned up his fiddle, homemade from sheep-gut and driftwood, and there was dancing. This would be followed by singing, the singers being called on in turn. Places were now taken round the fire and the *seanchaí*, or story-teller, began. By tradition the man of the house had the first right; others followed. They told tales of heroes like Fionn Mac Cumhail and his son Oisín (Macpherson's 'Ossian') with their roving warrior-band, the Fianna, one of the best known being the *Battle of Ventry*, when the Fianna defeated Dáire Donn, King of the World, not far from the Blasket Island. They told romantic, religious and humorous tales; myths, legends and tales of the supernatural. There were tales of local history such as those about the local poet-chieftain, Piaras Ferriter, whom the Islanders had sheltered after the unsuccessful rebellion of 1641. There were anecdotes too from the *seanchaí*'s own experience but shaped by his craft in the telling. In addition a vast number of international tales had found their way to this most remote corner of western civilization.

Out of the story-telling came the Blasket books. The craft was transferred to the printed page. From Peig's talk, and her son's pen, came the autobiographical *Peig*, 1936,[2] *An Old Woman's Reflections*, 1939,[3] the *Life of Peig Sayers*, 1970.[4]

Micheál had followed his brothers and sisters over to

---

[1] *Béaloideas*, the Journal of the Folklore of Ireland Society, 1975.
[2] Translated by Bryan MacMahon, Talbot Press, Dublin, 1974.
[3] Translated by Seamus Ennis, Oxford, 1962.
[4] Dublin, 1970, untranslated.

America but soon came back to resume the life he had left behind, at first on the Island, later in Dunquin. His evocation of life on the Blasket Island was inspired by Maurice O'Sullivan's *Twenty Years A-Growing*,[1] which had in turn been inspired by *The Islandman*. It is a literary curiosity how that book's author, Tomás O'Crohan, had been inspired by Russian literature: 'It would probably never have occurred to Tomás to write his life, had it not been for Mr. Brian O'Kelly of Killarney, who encouraged him to set about the work, and read over part of Maxim Gorki's autobiography to him to show the interest in that kind of writing.'[2]

Twenty Years A-Growing is a book of laughing youth. *A Pity Youth Does Not Last* takes the story to sombre middle age.

5

The Islanders had a unique character as a result of their isolation:

They had their own culture and a man from the Island could be picked out in any company. He can to this very day. This was a thing they brought out with them and a thing for which I have no proper name. It is neither shyness nor diffidence, though they are related to it; modesty, I suppose, is the nearest word to it, and any word you would have for an absence of rudeness. Where the man outside the Island would make a show of himself, the man inside would not.

Thus Pádraig Malone, grandson of Tomás O'Crohan.[3] His mother used to send him to sleep with bedtime stories of her youth on the Great Blasket, 'of the companionship and com-

[1] Translated by Moya Llewelyn Davies and George Thomson, Oxford, 1953.

[2] Foreword to Robin Flower's translation of *The Islandman*, Oxford, 1951.

[3] *Na hÁird ó Thuaidh*–'The Heights North'–Dublin 1960.

pany that were there and all the magic a person could see when the sun was setting'.

Micheál O'Guiheen describes some of that 'magic'. He describes the harshness of life too that in the twentieth century doomed an island which had neither doctor nor priest, grocery-pub nor post office. One cannot mourn the ending of a way of life that, especially in winter, was very bleak indeed; one cannot but mourn the ending of a culture that was rooted in the far distant past. In the Thirties the exodus grew, the young men and women heading mainly for America, the rest to live on the nearby mainland among Gaelic-speaking people whom they had known all their lives and to whom they were often related. In January 1942, shortly after finishing his book, Micheál O'Guiheen moved with Peig to where her parents had lived. The last of the Islanders were resettled on the mainland, with Government aid, in 1953. Peig died there at the age of 85 in 1958. Micheál, who remained a bachelor all his days, died in Dunquín on 27 April 1974, aged 70.

Micheál O'Guiheen who tells part of his story here – the part that mattered most to him – had, according to Professor Seamus Delargy, 'an accurate knowledge beyond the common of the history-lore of the Island and of the complexities of the Irish language.'[1] Bo Almqvist recalled him as 'my close friend, the first Irish story-teller I had the privilege to meet. He taught me, more than anyone else, about the folklore of Ireland.'[2]

So his lament is not for lost youth only, a theme as old as Homer's Nestor, but for the lost community of the Great Blasket Island. By implication he laments the breaking up, at an ever-increasing pace, of all such communities, closely knit

---

[1] *Seanchas ón Oileán Tiar* – 'Lore from the Western Island' – Dublin, 1956
[2] *An Béaloideas agus an Litríocht* – 'Folklore and Literature' – Cló Dhuibhne, 1977.

economically and culturally. Economically they may be no longer viable, but what about the rapid depletion of the world's cultural riches? Will the old Irish proverb prove true: *taréis a tuigtear gach beart* – we learn when it is too late?

TIM ENRIGHT

THE BLASKET GROUP
and
contiguous mainland.

Mount Brandon

PINGLE

Smerwick Harbour

BALLYDAVID

Sands Bay

MILLTOWN

Ferriter's Cove

BALLYFERRITER

Sybil Hd.

VENTRY

Ventry Harbour

Clogher Hd.

Croagh Marhin

CARHOO

DUNQUIN

Cooan

Mount Eagle

Carrig Valach

Beg-inish

Village

Slea Head

Blasket Sound

Inish Tuiscirt

Great Blasket

Wild Bank

BAY OF DINGLE

Great Sound

Teeraght

Inish na-Bro

Narrow Sound

Inish-vickillaun

Thunder Rock

Foze Rocks

Dingle to Tralee, 31 miles.
Dingle to Dublin, 238 miles.

Scale of Miles

0   1   2   3   4   5

STANFORD, LONDON

CHAPTER 1

Youth and School

MY love to God, isn't youth the grand thing! Isn't it a pity it doesn't stay with us always. But my sharp grief, it does not stay; the dark night slips down on the hills. I am a man who is getting on in years. It is many the hardship and trouble I suffered since I was twelve years of age until this day. But I give my thanks to God who helped me to go through it.

The place where I was born is the Great Blasket Island in the West of Ireland, the most westerly point in Ireland. It was there my father and mother married. All the land my father had was the grass of one cow. The luck of the world wasn't with him, for there was always something down on him that kept him very poor. I had three brothers and two sisters, Muiris, Pádraig, and Tomás, Cáit and Eibhlín. That was the number of our family that lived. My father was Pádraig O'Guiheen and Peig Sayers was my mother's name, a daughter of Tomás Sayers from Vicarstown. She was a quiet, honest woman and a good hardy woman too in her day.

I am the seventh in the family born to her and I was the unexpected stroke of luck. For this reason all the rest were fond of the little stranger that came into their midst. If the smoke of the fire blew on me they thought I was swept away from them. My sister Cáit wouldn't go anywhere without having me in her arms. When she went visiting to pass the night, she took me east with her to Seán Eibhlís's house, for it is there the small children of the village used to be gathered.

There was a crowd of children growing up on the Island at that time and they were the cross children. Cáit and Máire Sheáin Eibhlís used to have their books with them to learn their lessons for school and so would the rest of the youngsters who had the sense. When I grew tired of being there all I wanted was to be taken home. Cáit would be slow to leave the company, but she didn't want me to be in a sulk, so she used to take me in her arms.

Not long afterwards she took me with her to school. My heart was pounding in my breast with delight when the master gave me a new book. The master was a good hefty build of a man with a very healthy appearance on him. I didn't let go of the book but was looking at the nice pictures in it until midday. The door of the school was opened and out with the children.

'Let's be off home, astórín,' said Cáit, catching me by the hand at the school door.

When Cáit and myself went to school again, I had to stay with the babies while Cáit went to her own class. I was very frightened, for the other boys were staring at me, but Páidín Mhuiris whispered: 'I'll be your butty. I'm used to school and I'll help you.'

It was great ease to me when I heard him saying that much. After a while I noticed a big grown girl coming away from the table where the master was.

'Who's that grown girl, Páidín?' I whispered.

'That's the schoolmistress we have and a good mistress she is for she beats us only seldom.'

'She doesn't look cross, anyhow.'

She came over to us and took me by the hand.

'We've another little scholar today, God bless him.'

I hung my head with shame.

'Come on up, boy,' said she, 'and the master can put your name on the roll.'

I went with her. The master put my name on the roll and back I came again.

'Here you'll be from now on, little boy,' said the mistress and she put me sitting at the desk.

There were twenty-one children sitting on the bench in

front of me, every one of them having his own little book in his fist. I sat shyly in the middle, but I wasn't long there when I felt the shyness going from me. About five o'clock in the afternoon the master let us go home. Cáit took me by the hand at the school door and brought me away.

When I arrived home there was a grand pot of potatoes and pollock boiled by Mom, and I ate my fill of them.

'You were hungry, astórín,' she said.

My legs were bending with the weakness but I didn't care. I loved being at school. All the small children were there and we had great company. The master was pleasant. He was very gentle with me.

'The master is a fine honest man, pet, and a stranger in this place too.'

'And where's he from, Mom?'

'North of Tralee, some place. Tomás Savage is his name and it is the parish priest we have in Ballyferriter that found the school for him.'

'What's the name of the big woman going to school?' I asked.

'Cáit Manning is her name, astórín, the daughter of a good father and mother. It is north from Kilvickadownig she came.'

'I won't be afraid of her so.'

'There's no need to be, pet. There's no danger to anyone from that honest girl.'

I used to go to school every day from then on and I was doing fine. All the small boys used to gather at Seán Eibhlís's house at night; there we would be together learning our lessons.

Seán Eibhlís was a quiet, sensible man and a good scholar too. It was many the hard question he settled for us. He had three sons and two daughters. He never spoke a cross word to us, though it was often we gave him cause for it, for wherever the youth are gathered there's noise and commotion.

I was growing cute and smart as the days went by. I would often have to drive the cow home from the hill and draw the load of turf after school and many jobs the like of that. My father used to say that I was better off doing so than to be breaking my legs jumping from ditch to ditch.

CHAPTER 2

New Houses being built on the Island

ONE fine morning at the beginning of summer my brother
Pádraig and myself had to come home from school again. We
wanted money to buy new books. When we were making for
the house we saw all the people running down onto the
quay where a currach from Dunquin had landed with some
stranger.

'Holy Mary, Mom,' said I when I came home, 'there's a
stranger here from Dunquin whatever he wants. The whole
village is running down to meet him.'

'Yerra, pet, he's a clerk from the Board coming round
about the new houses that will be built any day now.'

'Will we have a new house, Mom?'

'We will, may it bring us luck, my son. I think six new
slate houses are going to be built straight away. I suppose it
was the money for the books that brought ye home from
school. I forgot it this morning. I had it here ready but ye
slipped out without so much as a word. Here it is now and
off with ye to school.'

Later in the day Diarmaid Thomáis , a next door neighbour of ours, called in and himself and my father started
chatting.

'Don't you think, Patsy,' says he to my father, 'that old
Paddy Guiheen's Well of the Ghost would make a nice site for
a house?'

'It would, I'd say, and it's on the right side and on a good
level. What would be his price for it, do you think?'

'The full of my hat of money he'd be wanting for it, man.
But I think if we gave him the Field of the Slab instead he'd
be satisfied.'

'Wisha, that the rogue may not grow fat on it,' said my father. 'It's good he is to himself! Isn't that the best field we have?'

'It is surely, but what remedy have we, since we're going to leave the old place. There's no other field I know better or more suited for a house to be built on it than Paddy's.'

'I suppose the clerk that came today will be making a start on the work as soon as possible.'

'He will, no doubt,' said Diarmaid, 'but it would take days to haul up the gravel in Shingle Strand. Their plan is to pay people to haul it up with asses.'

'That's slow work surely,' said my father.

'It is, man, but it will have to be done since that's the plan. What would come hardest on us would be finding carts to draw the gravel.'

'I suppose, Diarmaid, sacks would be no use for it.'

'Wisha, Patsy, that class of work is only a waste of time, going backwards and forwards on a long road with a little sack of gravel on your ass's back. You'd soon be cursing it. We'll have to find a cart some place or other.'

'That would be great, but we'll have to settle with old Paddy about the place first before we do anything else.'

'We'll have plenty of time for that at the start of the week. All Paddy wants is to make a swop for the other field and he'll be satisfied.'

The next Sunday my father went looking for a cart. He travelled far before he got one in the end from Pádraig Kavanagh in Clochar in Ballyferriter parish, on condition that he sent it back again when he was finished, or paid for any damage.

Yerra, man dear, it gave us a proper fright when my father put the cart on the ass. That was no wonder, since we had never before seen an ass's cart on the Island. It was all our noise till evening.

Said my father when he saw the state we were in: 'Ye've no sense, children. Have a bit of patience, ye're young yet, that's all. If ye've a long life ahead ye'll make little wonder of an old cart or of things far more important.'

He put three of us sitting inside the cart and drove the ass west along the road to the top of the strand. There wasn't a small child in the village but gathered before us west at the cross and my father had to find a place for them in the cart. He put no blame on them at all, he was only delighted.

When we came to where the men were working Seán Fada raised his head on hearing the noise making towards him.

'By the devil, Patsy, it's a cartload of youngsters you have! Wouldn't it have been far better for you altogether to have put a couple of good sacks of gravel on the cart when you were coming back east?'

'Oh, on my soul, but 'tis fine and easy for you to talk, Seán. These boys will do twice as much good for me yet with God's help.'

On the following Tuesday my father started drawing the gravel. He had no help, since his brother Micheál was hauling it up in Shingle Strand, so he had to keep my brother Muiris home from school. Muiris was slow to leave school, for it was just the time when he was starting to make headway with the learning. There was no way out of it, however, and in no time at all the pair of them had a big heap of gravel brought back. After school Pádraig and myself used to do many jobs and, whenever we got the chance, we paid a visit to the workmen. The site for our own house had been laid out and Seán Mhichíl and Tomás Dhónaill were mixing the gravel and cement.

'It won't be long now till ye're in the new house, children,' says Seán Mhichíl to us one day, shoving tobacco into his pipe.

'We won't all find room inside it, Seán Mhichíl,' says I.

'Ye will, boy. This will be the fine big house when 'tis finished. It only looks small now but wait, my lad, until you see it up.'

'We'll know when my father has the cow and the ass tethered at the side of the house as well as all the rest of us that are there. There won't be much empty space.'

'May God send us cause to laugh, gorsoon, what things come into yeer heads. There won't be a cow or an ass tethered inside this house of a night. Your father will have to put up a shed against the house for them.'

We used to be talking away with Seán Mhichíl until my father came east from the strand with his load of gravel. He would then take us back with him on the ass's cart, but we had to take to the road with our croobs of legs for the return journey, because of the big load he had always. He was trying to do extra before sending the cart back home.

Soon our new house was built and I'm telling you that the men didn't waste an hour and, if Seán Fada was a bit lazy itself, he had to put his back to the work. It is my father and mother that were the happy people to be able to go into a nice, dry, comfortable house where they could be free and easy for the rest of their lives.

We were all delighted to be leaving the horrible old hole, where we were smothered alive. However hard my mother tried to keep it clean and tidy she failed. Ourselves and Diarmaid's family moved house together. That's what my father wanted and Diarmaid Thomáis did his best to satisfy him.

CHAPTER 3

The Comet

WE weren't living in the new house long when a rumour went out among the people that a comet was to appear in the sky. The people were frightened of it. All they talked about from morning to night was the terrible star that was coming. The day was marked out when it would be here. Nobody expected he would have another day's life. That was the general story anyhow.

When the day for the great star to fall upon the world came, a big change took place while it was there. The day became night. When the master saw the day changing he said to the schoolmistress that it looked as if the story about the comet was no lie and he let the scholars go home. When my brother Tomás and myself came from school there was no one at home before us. My father was on the hill and the rest were around the village somewhere.

'Let's go, Tomáisín,' said I, 'to hide from the fire somehow. We've no business here on our own.'

Out with us in the middle of the storm and thunder and we went under a barrel at the side of the house. No one knew where we were until the storm was over. When we saw it tailing off we came out from under the barrel. We went in home and my father was after coming from the hill drowned wet. Everyone was frightened out of his life. No one looked his normal self. My mother had a bottle of holy water in her hand and was shaking it around the house.

'Great thanks be to God, children, that we're all safe together. Dickens a hope I had an hour ago that there would be anyone alive in the world, with all the noise that was there.'

'Little woman,' said my father, '"God is stronger than hope,"' and he took his hat from his head.

'I suppose, Patsy,' said she and her voice shaking, 'that those thunder claps did harm some place.'

'It is likely that someone is paying for them. The likes of them never fell so close without doing harm.'

As they were talking, in came Cáit O'Brien, the wife of the weaver. She was a great friend of my mother's and needn't fear to open her heart to her. Signs on, my mother was very fond of her.

'You're alive, Cáit,' said my father.

'That's about all, my dear man. I thought when the day became night that my life was at an end. It is often I saw lightning falling from the sky but I never before saw the likes of this and may God grant that I never see it again. Every thunderbolt was a mass of flame falling from the sky. May God save us from the fires of hell.'

'Amen,' said my father. 'But, Cáit O'Brien, wasn't it little dread the Dingle people had of it? Wasn't it well they came through the storm?'

'Yerra, let me alone with them, man; that fellow would do anything, to say he came on a day the likes of this.'

'Who's that?' I asked.

'Pádraig Brosnahan,' said my father. 'He was coming over the sea during the storm with a load of cement and timber.'

'God be with us,' said I, 'aren't they the brave strong people in Dingle. Isn't it hard to put fear in them.'

'Oh pet, they had the load in the trawler and when they got the wind they put out. The poor men never expected the change would be so sudden. But there's nothing lost by it, thanks be to God.'

'Yerra, Patsy, if you only saw old Micil Keane and the tough job he had putting the donkey's straddle-mat up against the window trying to keep out the red shadow of the flashes!'

'I suppose the poor man was afraid, Cáit. Micil isn't well for a long time.'

'I'm telling you, Patsy, and believe me too, that everyone else was afraid along with him. Look at Eibhlís Mhór for instance, though, according to herself, she's the great soldier. She had a picture of the Virgin Mary while going from her mother's house to her own.'

'It was a good thing she had, my dear woman, if she had the proper trust in the Mother of God in her heart.'

'I suppose she had, Patsy, for she had the rosary along with it.'

'It will be a long time before the likes of this day will come again.'

'May it never come again with God's will, we've trouble enough as it is.'

'We have, wisha, Cáit, you're right,' said my father and he left us with his pipe reddened and didn't return to the house again before night.

Next morning the din was gone. The sky was clear and bright and one would think there had never been any anger on it. There was a great difference between the two days, a hundred thanks to God. People were working again as well as ever. Nobody was trembling with dread. All the great fright and olagóning and wringing of hands was on one side.

'Faith, today will be the great day for work altogether,' said my father.

'I suppose it will, dear,' said my mother, answering him.

'By my palms it will,' said he. 'It will take a while to put away the great load of timber that was in the trawler, not to mention all the cement.'

'I thought there was no need for any more cement, that all the new houses were nearly finished.'

'There's a little bit to do to them yet. It will be a while before they are finished with them, anyhow.'

'It will, I suppose. The longer the work is there the better it is for the men. The money will be growing day by day.'

'You're right in that much, little woman. There's no limit to it for money. It is early in the morning Seán Fada is down below on the quay working, though he's the tough, lazy man.'

'I don't blame him. It isn't always the poor man will get a chance to earn a shilling.'

'It is not indeed. A man is in a poor way without it. What I'm thinking about now is to go down amongst the men. Maybe I'd be able to earn some sixpence. Our son Muiris will do the work of the house instead of me and the little lads, Micil and Páidín, will bring the turf home from the bog after school. They wouldn't be better off gallivanting east and west.'

'They would not. There's a great danger to them! The likes of them are everywhere doing jobs.'

My father stood up and put his hat on his head.

'May the day bring you luck,' said my mother.

When my father was gone out a while myself and my two brothers, Pádraig and Tomás, went to school. That was the very day beyond all days in the world that the inspector came. He was a middle-aged man with two great, bulging, shining eyes in him. He hadn't a word of Irish in his puss. But to our misfortune he had plenty of English. He put many questions to us. On my soul we had no jizz left when he was finished with us.

When the inspector was gone the master and mistress went to talk to one another. They were whispering for a while, then the master spoke:

'Well, children, I'm very thankful to ye. Ye did well by me today. The inspector himself was very pleased with ye, ye did so well. I suppose ye'd be glad if I gave ye half a day's holi-day now.'

'We would, master,' said Muiris Kearney.

'I don't begrudge it to ye, Muirisín, and welcome,' and he let us out home from school.

I had the rest of the day at my ease looking at the workmen. My father was there working skilfully amongst them. I saw no trace of Seán Fada in any direction and I asked my father where was he.

'On my soul, boy, it won't be long till he's here. He's drawing timber poles up to the road to Seán Mhichíl and the Yank and they're putting them standing.'

'I suppose, Dad, 'tis hard work.'

'Not at all, son. There's no one complaining more than Seán Fada.'

'And why is he complaining, Dad?'

'Wisha, I don't know, pet, a bit of his old cuteness, I suppose.'

Seán Fada came on, gabbing away, but Paddy O'Crohan told him to give up his old chat and do something; that he had been talking like that since morning and should be ashamed of himself.

'I'm hoarse from blathering,' said Seán.

'If you weren't such a chatterbox you wouldn't be hoarse,' said my father.

'He wouldn't, Patsy, you're right there,' said Paddy O'Crohan. 'But the devil himself wouldn't make the man used to talking stay quiet.'

It wasn't long till the great heap of timber was drawn up to the top of the village. Neither Seán Mhichíl nor the Yank was idle. It was many the strong belt they gave with the sledge hammer before the last pole was put standing. The crowd that were doing the drawing up to them weren't idle either. It was the heavy tread they had coming home in the evening.

CHAPTER 4

The Day of the Auction on the Island

THERE was a great commotion among the Islanders for it was
an auction day. All the wood, left over after the new houses
were finished, was being auctioned off. Tomás Mór was our
auctioneer. There wasn't a boy or man in the village but was
there, for what is rare is wonderful. Not many of them had
ever seen an auction before. Tomás Mór picked up a piece of
timber and gave it great praise.

'Well, men,' said he, 'anyone with money mustn't be back-
ing away. Now is the time for him. He has the makings of a
table or a ladder here out of the finest timber to be got. Don't
be shy, Yank, man. Come over here. You've been saying for a
week that you badly needed the makings of a ladder. Here it
is for you now, man. Make your bid. If you let it go to anyone else and it here for you, you'll always be regretting it.

'Seán Fada, is there any shift out of you? Weren't you looking out too for the makings of a table? Ye'll be looking for it
when I won't have it to give, maybe.'

'Tomás,' says my father, 'I'll take the makings of a big
ladder here away with me.'

'On my soul, Patsy, but you're the man with the gumption.
Take it away with you, boy.'

My father put his hand in his pocket and gave three shillings for it. Tomás spat on the money and put it in his pocket.
My father started the battle, for from then on everyone was
buying until there wasn't enough timber left to boil a kettle
for an old woman.

Tomás Mór was well satisfied after the day. Why wouldn't
he be? Hadn't he good pay out of being an auctioneer?

The Yank was very vexed because my father had swept off

the ladder, but my father was too clever for him and had slipped in ahead.

My father was one of those who bought the most wood that day. He needed it, for he was going to put up a new room and since the timber was going so cheap he decided to buy it. He said that a man would spend twice as much going to Dingle for it.

When the auction was over the young lads had great fun below on the strand. They had small boats made of cork and were putting them to sail on the water. I need hardly say that I wouldn't be satisfied without being in the middle of them, and having my own share of sport as well as anyone. Off down with me at a gallop. But I declare to you I wasn't but below at the water's edge when my boot slipped on a stone and I fell on top of my head into the sea.

When I came to the surface, the sense was knocked out of me with the fright I got. When the other lads saw me falling into the water they ran off up the path in a panic. They called Tomás Dhónaill and my brother Muiris. Down they came racing. Tomás Dhónaill had an oar and he stretched it out to me, but I hadn't the wit to catch hold of it. When my brother saw the danger I was in he didn't wait to take off boot or sock but jumped in after me. The water was up to his own neck, but he didn't care so long as he had a grip of me. Himself and Tomás Dhónaill took me up with them.

'On my soul, Muiris,' said Tomás Dhónaill, shoving tobacco in his pipe, 'if we had laughter and fun this morning, it was close we went to having a sad evening of it.'

'I suppose, Tomás Dhónaill,' said Muiris, 'it was the God of Glory, may He be praised for ever, that made us stay behind at the top of the quay after the rest. If we had gone home, my brother would have been drowned and what would we do then?'

'It has every appearance of it,' said Tomás Dhónaill. 'Sure there wasn't a thing to save him.'

My heart was trembling for fear my mother would hear the story, but nobody told her. It was in Diarmaid Thomáis's house I dried my clothes with a fine turf fire that was there. When I thought they were dry enough I came home. It was a long time afterwards before I went anywhere near the quay. I was well able to look after myself, anyhow, before I went there.

There's nothing like learning the hard way.

CHAPTER 5

Living in the new House

SOON after we went to live in the new house my mother had to go home to Dunquin. She preferred to be with her mother in a case of that sort. She thought it was the best place for her to get what she needed. My father had to gather a crew for a currach. The poor men didn't mind going along with him at all; 'twas how they were tripping over one another.

My mother wasn't long in Dunquin when she had a baby daughter. That was the baby, reader, that we had the welcome for, I'm telling you. It seemed like ages to us till our mother would be home again and the small stranger with her. We were counting the days, but she came in the end with the baby in her arms. We all kissed the baby dotingly and then my mother put Eibhlín Óg to sleep in the cradle.

My mother wasn't up and about again when the women of the village gathered in to see the baby and have the crack with her after her journey. But when my father, who was sitting in the corner, heard the women faulting the child, he jumped up raging.

'Wisha, morning's croak on ye, if it isn't hard to please ye! That little child is the way God made her, praise be to Him for ever. May the person amongst ye that will find fault with her have red eyes!'

The women pulled in their horns with shame because they had been talking gibberish. Not one of them stayed. They scuttled out fast and old Nell too stirred herself to go.

'Let you stay, Nell,' said my father. 'Aren't you one of ourselves, sure?'

He went down to the room and brought a bottle of whiskey up with him and filled out a good glass of it.

'Here,' said he, 'let you have that much, Nell, out of the christening.'

'O God of Miracles, Patsy, is it how you want people to be making sport of me? Half of that will do you.'

'It will not, Nell; drink it back and may God grant us all a long, happy life of it.'

'Amen,' said Nell, wiping her mouth with her apron.

CHAPTER 6

How I got Thrush

A COUPLE of years after we moved house the thrush came on me and my mother had to take me out to Dunquin. There was an old woman in Móinteán at the time and she had the cure for this disease. Méireas was her name and she was married to a weaver by the name of Seán Keating. They had a small, dry, sheltered house on the edge of the cliff. Méireas was a pleasant, lively woman and a woman with a big heart too. She told my mother she wouldn't have had to go to the trouble of bringing me to Dunquin if she'd known about it.

'How so, Méireas?'

'Wisha, Peig, if ye had any white gander at home and put him under a creel till morning; and then if you opened the little boy's mouth and let the gander breathe down well into his throat, I guarantee you there wouldn't be a trace of the disease left in your little boy.'

'Oyeh, honest woman, "the fur on the cat looks glossy"! We hadn't a gander, black or white, in the village, no matter if our salvation from the fires of hell depended on him.'

'I suppose so, my dear,' said Méireas. 'I heard that no goose would stay on the Island.'

'They do not. Sure I had a grand flock of them myself one time, but the devil a one I have now. The same thing happened to them as happened to Mór's[1] wealth long ago.'

---

[1] The reference is to a folk-tale. Mór, defying her father, a man of substance, marries Donnchadh Dee who is poor. Love wanes and, regretting her lost wealth, Mór becomes a shrew. One day, when the long-suffering Donnchadh is sent to gather firewood, St. Brendan appears and offers him two wishes as a reward for his patience. Donnchadh, a simple man, cannot make up his mind what to ask for and decides to consult Mór. On his way back, weary from his load, he sits down saying 'I wish I were home.' He is lifted

I darted a glance down towards the bottom of the house and saw the pair in the room below, working away hard. They were weaving with two looms. Old Keating was a clever weaver and his daughter Máire was every scrap as good. Why wouldn't she be? Wasn't her father able to give her the good teaching?

When Máire Keating saw myself and my mother she left her work and came up to welcome us. That was no wonder, for she had no friend she preferred before my mother when the two of them were young. You would think that it was down out of the heavens we came to her, she was so delighted to see my mother.

'How long is the little lad complaining with that disease, Peig?' she said.

'With a week, my dear, and the devil a bit of notice I took of it, but on my oath it was getting worse this rogue was. I was told to take him with me quickly out to Méireas, so when I found the day fine I brought him out.'

'It was well you did. He'll come to no harm with God's help,' said Méireas. 'But you'll have to leave him here along with me for three days.'

'I was going to go up to Vicarstown.'

'All right, so, Peig, but don't forget to bring the little boy down to me in the morning fasting.'

'Wouldn't it be better for him to stay here with ourselves,' said Seán Keating, 'until the cure would be made?'

'It's up to themselves,' said Méireas. 'It isn't any cold welcome there is here for them.'

---

through the air and to his own house. Mór, when she learns the story, rounds on Donnchadh for so foolishly wasting a wish. At last in exasperation Donnchadh exclaims 'I wish the length of Ireland were between us!' Mór with her family is lifted through the air to a cabin in Dunquin, the nearest house in the western world to America. Donnchadh lands in the North East of Ireland, the nearest point to Scotland. Mór becomes a beggar in the latter end of her days.

Great Blasket Village

Micheál O'Guiheen seated (centre) with Maurice O'Sullivan (melodeon) and friends on the Great Blasket, 1924.

'Thank you, Méireas, there's no need for it. My own people have a long, wide house above in Vicarstown. We'll stay there from now till Sunday; isn't there a great danger to me walking down here in the morning! I'd go farther from home to get a cure for my son.'

'So it seems, my good woman,' said Seán Keating, ' "The one the shoe pinches feels it." Maybe the little lad is hungry?'

'By my palms, he won't be hungry long,' said Máire Keating, and she put white bread and milk heating in a big saucepan on the fire. When it was fine and warm, the way she wanted it, she made me swallow every bit.

When we were getting up to leave, Máire Keating wouldn't let my mother stir from her, by hook or by crook, without having the drink of tea along with them. It was then the crack started in earnest, the two of them gossiping about the great deeds they did together in their young days.

The day was well on when we made out Vicarstown. It was my first journey ever to the house of my grandparents. Myself and my mother were walking along the road at our ease. We were in no hurry, for we were suffering neither from hunger nor anything else. She was pointing the place out to me. We sat down by the side of the road where we had a grand view. It was a lovely evening and a very interesting sight to see. The great wide ocean was without a stir in any direction, but smooth as a dice. The sun itself at the time was going down in the shadow of Barra Lia. A person looking back on the sea that evening would think there was molten gold on the water, the colour was so bright.

'Mom,' said I, 'what's the name of that great hill there beyond?'

'That's Mount Eagle, child. That mountain was full of eagles in my young days, though there isn't one of them left now. There is a great lake on top of it and there used to be an eagle's nest in the cliff above the lake. But it is a long time now since there was any eagle's nest there. A doctor from

Dingle it was that bought the last one of them from a woman in the parish of Ventry.'

'And how did she get hold of it, Mom? Isn't the eagle a very strange bird?'

'Well, child, the eagle is a very wary bird, without a doubt, but what the woman from the parish of Ventry did was to creep up on it. One fine summer's day she was up on top of the hill. There wasn't a puff of wind out of the sky and she saw the eagles washing themselves in the lake. She crept up on them and flung the shawl from her head over them. One went under it. When she twisted the shawl round him, the eagle drove his claw into the palm of her hand and out through the other side. The poor woman screamed and screeched. By the devil, wasn't her husband putting a clamp on a rick of turf and didn't he hear her. He ran towards her, for the poor man didn't know what was up, but when he saw the eagle and the claw stuck in the hand of his wife, he nearly dropped dead with the fright. If he killed himself trying, he couldn't pull out the eagle's claw. The poor woman had to go to the doctor in Dingle. I think he had to cut the eagle's claw to loosen its grip.'

'God save us, Mom, she suffered great pain.'

'She did, child. She had to suffer great pain before the doctor was able to draw the eagle's claw out. But the doctor gave her her fare for the road home, for he bought the eagle from her.'

It was well on into the evening when myself and my mother walked into my grandparents' house.

'God bless my soul, ye're welcome,' said Cáit Boland.

We knocked a start out of her, for she had no notion we were going to come at that hour of the evening. Cáit was a fine, tidy woman and a woman that had a big heart.

'Long life to you, Cáit,' said my mother. 'How're ye all since?'

'We mustn't complain, dear, so long as we have the health. What's on the little boy, Peig?'

'Wisha, Cáit, he's complaining about his little mouth. He has it sore for a while. I had him below with Méireas and she said the thrush was on him.'

'Oh, if that's what's on him, he'll come to no harm, with God's help. The kettle is on the hob; it won't be long now. I'll go and call Seán for the tea. He's back at Eoghan Browne's house. I won't make any delay,' and she went off in a rush back across the river.

I sat on a little stool beside the fire. There was a grand fire sending heat around the house and a settle-bed in the corner with my grandfather sleeping in it. There he preferred to be, because he didn't have the use of his legs and somebody or other was always coming in and out. It gave him great peace of mind to be chatting with them.

When he saw myself and my mother he was so overcome that he couldn't speak a word to us. But when the fit passed, he was talking away from then on.

Three mornings, one after the other, my mother took me down to Méireas. I knew them all so well in the end that you would have thought I was born amongst them. When my Uncle Seán would tell me to go down to the Field of the Stack and drive the cow back up, I'd do it gladly. I used to carry a bucket of water back from the river to Cáit Boland and do many jobs for them the like of that.

But on the Sunday my father came to fetch us. I had a great longing to go back home to my own house. Before I left, I went over to the bed where my grandfather was and said goodbye to him.

'The blessing of God go with you, my little love,' said he; 'may God bring ye safe home.'

Then myself and my mother walked back to the top of the cliff. Father stayed behind after us in Vicarstown. There was no hurry on him for the day was fine and we were a good while on top of the cliff waiting for him.

Then we came back home to the Island.

CHAPTER 7

The Mackerel Season

'ON my soul, Seán,' my father said to Seán Fada, 'there's every sign of fish in the sea today.'

'There is, Patsy. The gannets are there, whatever, if it's mackerel they have.'

'Yerra, what else would they be tearing to pieces, man, but mackerel?'

'Faith, Patsy, 'tis often I saw gannets diving just as hard, but it wouldn't be a great deal of fish you'd kill.'

'Tutt, man! The boats will be filled up with them tonight. Sure that sight of gannets back there would stop anyone grumbling, all thanks and praise to our Holy Lord that sent them to us.'

'There's no fault on that sight, Patsy; they'll put a shilling into the pocket of many a poor man.'

'That's true, Seán. There's many a man jumping with joy today when he sees the gannets diving. "Every fosterchild follows its rearing and the duck takes to the water". That's how it is with us and the fish; 'tis our way of life.'

'You're right there, Patsy, but I don't think tonight will make a night for the fishing. I was up on Mullachrowar this morning for a load of turf and you'd see clearly a man standing in Inish-vickillaun.'

'That's no good sign for weather, Seán. But if we haven't this night itself for fishing, we'll have another night, with God's help. It is a great thing that the fish have come to the place. Ho O! What's up with those people east there now, Seán, that they're running?'

'My soul from the devil, Patsy, I don't know. I suppose it's some stranger that has come to the village.'

'It is, Dad,' said I, 'a currach has come into the quay now and 'tis full of strangers.'

'Faith, but what a time they picked, as Seán Phaid said to Betty[1] long ago. I wonder what brought them up here?' my father said.

'On my word, Patsy, if they were hearty enough setting out, I'm afraid they won't have much of it left at the latter end of the day.'

Seán Fada was right, for they were only out making for Beg-inish Point on the way home when it blew from the North-East. The wind was getting stronger and white ripples coming over the sea.

'Would you say, Patsy, that there's any danger of the little currach?' Pats Tom asked my father.

'I'd say there is, Pats. If they're driven further out to sea they won't ever again reach Beg-inish Little Cove.'

You'd think the currach was a black crow at the time, with the way the sea was being churned up all around it.

'The poor men will be lost, so,' said Pats Tom.

'I'm afraid they will,' my father said, 'unless some help can be sent after them.'

'If I could get three more that would follow me, I'd go after them,' said Pats Tom.

'That God may not take away the power from your limbs. We were never without brave men on the Island,' said my father.

'I'll go with you,' said Seán Fada.

'God be with you, Seán,' said my father. 'Good never went astray on anyone.'

Two more followed them. It was soon they had the currach afloat and away with it across the waters of the sea, back towards Beg-inish, with white spray being whipped up by the wind behind them.

---

[1] Betty Rice, the local landowner.

'May God bring their own back safe and well to everyone,' said my mother. 'It looks as if it's a bad case entirely.'

'It does, Peig,' said Nell Mhór, 'but God is strong and he has a good mother.'

The Island currach was going ahead fine until Seán Fada broke a thole-pin. That put great delay on them, but Seán found a big iron thole-pin.

'I declare to goodness,' he said, 'that any boat is lost without the likes of these thole-pins in it,' and he started pulling away again.

'Men,' said Pats Tom, 'let ye not lose heart at all. A couple of strokes more and the job will be done by us, along with the help of God. The Dunquin currach is below between me and Beg-inish Point and she's making no headway at all. Have the rope ready, Máirtín, to throw to them when we draw near.'

'Don't let that bother you, Pats,' said Máirtín, 'the rope is in the right place still.'

'Let us pass windward of them, Pats,' said Seán Fada.

'We will if we can, Seán,' said Pats.

Máirtín threw the rope and landed it in the middle of the Dunquin currach.

It was the Dunquin people that were glad when they caught hold of the end of the rope. It was help at the right time, for the poor men were worn out and not able to give another stroke. When they came to the quay of the Island, there was back-slapping, shouting and clapping hands.

'Give over yeer useless old gibberish, women and children,' said Nell Mhór, 'but let us first give thanks from our hearts to God who brought the men home safe to us out of the danger they were in.'

'Faith, my honest woman, but that's the talk with the sense to it and isn't it the blather without shape or make to it that these have,' said Pats Mór. 'Come on, men,' he said to the strangers.

It was soon that the memory of the sea and the terrible

fright and the echo of the waves and the lonely whistling of the wind in their ears was slipping away from them. Pats Mór was the right man to scatter the gloom of the sea from them with the grand flattering tongue he had. The poor men went out home next day.

From then on the mackerel were being killed and the people of the Island were making good money on them.

CHAPTER 8

A Day's Hunting and Peevishness

I HAD a little holiday and I wanted to make the most of it, so I sat outside on the ditch in the open air. The weather was lovely and the sun shining pleasantly on everything. I could hear the noise of the waves breaking on the sand of the shore. The birds were hopping gaily from ditch to ditch. I was delighted in my heart to be listening to them, because for a week I had a poor chance of seeing anything like that since I used to be at school.

'Well,' says I in my own mind, 'I'll have a good day today, whatever.'

Before we'd eaten our breakfast Páidín Mhuiris, with his hunting dogs at his heels, came to call for me.

'Are you coming?' he asked.

'I am if I'm let,' said I.

'You will be let, on my word,' said my father, 'but don't have the misfortune to go into any dangerous place.'

When I heard my father saying that much, my heart was jumping with joy.

The day was very warm and neither Páidín nor myself was performing any great feat with the rabbits. Stretched out on clumps of heather under the sun was how we spent most of the day.

'I'd better go and gather the full of my cap of gulls' eggs,' Páidín said, 'for I've nothing else going home.'

'There's nothing to stop us,' said I. 'We're in the right place for it.'

Off down with us to Biddie's Point to make a start on the work. Páidín was in front of me with his cap in his hand. We weren't long filling the two caps with eggs for there was a seagull's nest on the hollow of every rock there.

When we had enough of them gathered, we headed for the top. The place was full of cracks and we had to be very careful in case our boots got caught in the deep cracks cut into the rocks by age and weather.

'Take care of yourself, whatever, Páidín,' said I, 'for the place is very slippery.'

'It is too, faith, but don't mind that, we're nearly at the top of the cliff now.'

It is said that "there's no joy without sorrow to go with it," for Páidín had hardly finished speaking when his boot got caught in one of the cracks.

'Holy Mary, Holy Mary, I'm stuck!' said he.

'Take it easy, Páidín, "the help of God is nearer than the door."'

I put the cap that I was holding away neatly in a good safe place and went to where Páidín was stuck.

'God give me help,' said I, and I caught him by the collar of his coat. 'Bend down as far as you can till you reach your boot,' said I. 'Rip the lace on it and draw out your foot.'

I had hold of Páidín like an eagle would have hold of a young lamb. When he ripped the lace in his boot, the foot came free. He was so delighted that he didn't bother to bring the boot up with him. I had to go down myself to pull it out. I didn't let on that there was anything out of the way.

When I reached home, it wasn't any praise my father heaped on me for the work of the day. It was how he smashed all the gulls' eggs I had, but one, on the stone outside the door.

'It wouldn't take much to make me do the same with that one,' he said, 'but it has ever been said that "a child wants to have everything he sees and likes." Let there be an end to this class of work, boy, or there will only be either yourself or myself in this house.'

I was as vexed as a roasted herring, but I knew well my father was right and that all he was doing was frightening me off.

CHAPTER 9

Shrovetide and the great Commotion

PEOPLE are very fidgety during Shrovetide. That's no wonder, for there's many a man wants to settle himself well. It
isn't only in this village that people get restless, but in every
townland from Mór's house to the house of Donnchadh Dee.[1]
People have stored away a nice purse of money to give their
daughters and sons a good start and foundation.

There's all the hugger-mugger in the world going on during Shrovetide. Of course the old women aren't idle. Chatter
lifts the dullness of their days from them. The old women of
the Island aren't satisfied without having their own share of
the same chatter, as long as anyone can remember them.

'It is high time for Páid here below to make some shift to
settle himself. Sure he has the back teeth well by this time,'
my mother said to Nell Mhór one evening.

'Oyeh, wisha, my dear, it is high time surely for him to be
making some stir for himself from now on, but he hadn't the
chance till now,' said Nell.

'Máire Shéamaisín is the woman, I suppose, Nell.'

'She is surely, Peig; a quiet, sensible, self-respecting girl.'

'That describes her perfectly. No one need teach her. I'm
telling you that Máire is the very woman to go about her
business properly.'

'It is no blather or foolishness poor Páid has now,' said
Nell. 'He's holding the young woman by the hand and having the great talk, saying he's the man that's able to keep her
properly. You'd think he'd give her a kiss in front of her
mother, they're that fond of each other.'

'They've the match made, so, Nell.'

[1] See footnote, p. 19.

'I dare say they have, Peig. Séamaisín, the young woman's father, was in great fettle and singing "White Wandering Rose" nice and soft and sweet. The poor fellow had a drop taken.'

'Good himself! 'Tis long since the poor man could drink his heart's fill of it. Ha-Ha, girl, that's the laddo that can make him sing Dónall-na-Gréinne.'

'Wisha, I don't know, Peig, the person that never tasted it is as well off. All that's in it is a kick for that while only.'

'Do you know for certain when the couple are marrying, Nell?'

'Shrove Tuesday is the day they've picked.'

'Good luck to them,' my mother said.

The night before Shrove Tuesday Páid didn't forget to invite his relations to his wedding. He left no one in the village that he didn't put to a refusal. The grown-up boys and girls were getting themselves ready for the day. My sister Cáit and my brother Muiris were going and they were in raptures, I'm telling you.

'On my word, wisha, my dear children, there's no need for ye to be so eager, for "going to the king's palace is not the same as coming from it." If ye were said by me, ye'd stay home.'

'Don't mind that, Patsy,' said my mother. 'Give them their head and don't be knocking them off their stride. There's great danger to them! These will leg it north and back again as well as the rest of their likes in the village that are going there. They'll be a burden to no one. They have their own good, strong, sound legs for the road.'

'You're right, little woman, but all the same you'd never know when those young buckoes might turn home. Maybe, woman, 'twould be in the middle of the night that the thought would cross their minds to head back and it is no nice time for a little ball of a girl to be traipsing after a lad in the middle of the night. But I won't stop her if she wishes to go.'

'God bless you, Dad,' said Cáit and she gave every puck-jump around the floor with delight.

The following morning there wasn't a currach in the Island that hadn't gone out to Dunquin. My father went too, despite all his remarks the night before about the people going there. My sister Cáit went with him. He wouldn't let her go with anyone else for fear they wouldn't look after her too well when they got a bit airy. My father was very understanding about things like that.

There were several weddings in Ballyferriter that day. Páid and Máire Shéamaisín were the first to marry. People were saying that it was a long time since a couple as handsome got married in Buailtín chapel.

When Páid returned home in the evening it wasn't empty he came. He had the grain of tea with him to make punch for the old women and I'm telling you he got blessings if anyone ever got them before. If luck was wished on him once, it was wished on him a thousand and seven hundred times. He didn't leave the old men short of drink either. They had their drop swallowed back. There was white bread and tea in plenty there, not to mention music and dancing.

When the young lads and girls that were at the wedding returned, it wasn't for home they made, but for the gathering-house. When Cáit and Páid arrived they made no delay at home but off with them to the wedding-feast. Myself and Páidín Mhuiris were there from the start of the night. We were comfortable above in the corner. When the people of the village gathered in in the course of the evening Bríde, Páid's mother, was very busy tidying the house for the wedding-feast. She sent some of the lassies that were old enough onto the strand for dry sand, so that she could have it to sprinkle on the floor.

She removed the old lamp hanging on the wall and put another there instead. She washed and cleaned the table in the kitchen. The cow and ass were put into an old shed at the gable end of the house. Old Pádraig said that was the best place for them to be; they had no business taking up room, for the house would be small enough without them when the crowd would gather.

He was right, for when the crowd arrived there wasn't enough room for a little mouse, though that's a paltry animal to mention. The boys and young girls weren't too happy for they hadn't enough room to dance. But there was no cure for it. The house was too small and too many people there. Late in the night Bríde, the mother of the young man, whispered to my sister Cáit:

'Cáitín, call Máire Sheáin Eibhlís, ye're the youngest and ye're the best to make the tea and put the kitchen things out on the table.'

'On my soul, Bríde, we wouldn't prefer to be idle,' said Cáit and she called Máire Sheáin Eibhlís.

The room door had to be taken down and four big boxes put under it in the middle of the house, for the table was too small, with not enough room for everybody round it.

It wasn't long till I was falling asleep and my brother Muiris had to take me home. He went off himself again and a hurry on him for fear he might miss any bit of the sport.

It was broad daylight when the people left the house of the wedding-feast.

CHAPTER 10

Bad News – The Death of Nell Mhór's little Girl

WHEN I got up next morning there was no good news for me to hear. Nell Mhór's lovely little girl was dead. A sudden fit she got and she died, with no expectation of it. Poor Nell Mhór was breaking her heart out crying and the women of the village were consoling her. It was very hard for the poor woman to be said by them. She was sitting on her haunches and the marks of sorrow were stamped on her features. The master didn't open the school at all that day, because a little girl was dead in the village.

According as a man would come into Nell Mhór's he would sit down quietly without a sound. The child was laid out nicely in a cradle at the side of the house in such a way that a person would think she was having a peaceful sleep.

My father and Micil, the child's father, were below in the room making the coffin. She wasn't going to have any funeral as she was so young.

When the sun set in the evening, she was taken away down to Castle Point. My father went into Seán Fada's house looking for a spade. Seán Fada helped him and they dug a hole and placed her in it.

'It is the bitter pity,' said my mother, 'that we aren't all as clean from sin as that little angel here today. Her state in heaven is lovely.'

'True for you, Peig,' Bríde answered, 'but our will isn't God's will.'

'That it may not be so, Bríde. If Nell Mhór had her wish, Máirín wouldn't be lying under these sods here.'

'She wouldn't, wisha, Peig, and may God not punish me for saying it, but she'd be better off to have Máirín alive to fetch a bucket of water to her from the well.'

'Let you have God's love in your heart, Bríde, isn't she better off to possess a place in God's kingdom.'

'You're right, Peig. There's no place better for Nell Mhór to have her child than in heaven, since it fell to her lot,' said Cáit Mhór. 'Shake yourself up, Nell, and don't be crying. She's gone from you now. God took her to Himself, praise be to Him for ever. You'll be glad yet, Nell, when Máirín will come looking for you and a little light in her hand to guide you on the long road of eternity.'

'God help us, Cáit, amn't I destroyed entirely, the one little darling that I had, and my heart was wrapped up in her, to be swept out of my arms, with no thought of it. I had no notion but that God would leave that little girl to watch over me when I died. But look at how the story is now. I'll have a dark, black, sad life of it for the rest of my days.'

'The grace of patience to you, you poor woman,' Cáit said.

'You have enough of them yet with God's help,' said my mother, 'if God lets them live for you.'

'It is a good hen that keeps the whole clutch,' said Cáit, standing up. 'We've no business in this graveyard here talking. We'll be long enough here when we're dead.'

The people of the village sympathized with Nell Mhór that night. They kept her company until morning.

A wedding and a wake took place together in the village.

CHAPTER 11

The Great War

A COUPLE of years after the marriage of Páid and Máire Shéamaisín the great war in France began. Vessels were being sunk all over the ocean. At that time a big ship ran aground at Lóchar Rock on the north side of the Island. There wasn't a man or woman in the village who wasn't knocked sideways with the awful fright they got when they saw the fine vessel and her masts hanging over the water so near to their homes.

I had my head down writing at my bench in the school-house when I heard all the row and tatarrara outside. I looked up and stared out, but saw no one except the Yank, with his thole-pins in his hands, running down the road. He gave every puck-jump like a kid goat and every now and then he would look daggers at someone following at his heels.

I made out there were extraordinary goings-on some place since the Yank was that way, for he was no scatter-brain, whatever other faults he had. We were waiting then till someone might come by to tell us what was up. The master was as little in the know as anyone else. But we hadn't a long wait of it, for Cáit Mhicil came towards us down the glen. The master asked her what was disturbing the people to be carrying on like that.

'Well, master,' she said, 'there isn't an old woman or a young woman above in the village that hasn't gone back to Seal Cove Point.'

'What do they want back there?' he asked in wonder.

'There's a ship wrecked at Lóchar Rock and the fishermen are like to drown one another round it.'

'By my palms, that wouldn't be strange at all. "What is rare is wonderful."'

He went to converse with the schoolmistress. It was very hard to make him out with the fretting that was on him.

'Well,' said he, ''tisn't long from "time" and since the afternoon is fine we'll go to look at the sport.'

Off with us back the road, the master at the head and ourselves behind, and we made neither stop nor stay till we reached Seal Cove Point. There wasn't the width of my palms of the open sea that wasn't covered with wreckage.

'Wisha the curse of God and His Holy Church on it for a vessel,' said Bríde, ''tis how she'll drown the men. Look at the tussling among them over old articles not worth a Jew's harp without a tongue.'

'You're right, Bríde,' said my mother. 'They're like to drown one another over her. If they had any sense, sure, there was plenty entirely there.'

'There was too, woman, but no one has ever enough sense. It is learning a person is all through his life.'

'On my word, men,' said Seán Fada, 'whatever greed was on us in the morning for it, we have enough of it now.'

'Thanks be to God, Seán,' the Yank said, 'isn't plenty the grand thing. We have our heart's content of it in the heel of the hunt.'

'Some of ye were hard enough to satisfy,' said Seán, 'but ye have the greed knocked out of yeer hearts now.'

There wasn't a morning for a month afterwards that you would not see some currach or other passing the Spur from the west, and it piled high with wreck. But on my word it was soon the day came when a currach passed the Spur from the West and no wreck at all in it.

'"It isn't every day that Dónall Buí is marrying or can make the arrangements,"' said my father when he heard that the currach had come back empty.

'On my oath, it will fall hard on the poor now to come

The Great Blasket

down in the world,' said my mother.

'We were used to tasty mouthfuls for a good while, little woman.'

'We were, man, but I suppose we'll be on the spare again from now on.'

'I'm afraid we'll have to be sparing with many things. 'Tis said, if it's true, that there isn't a stone of flour to be found in any shop in Dingle.'

'God bless my soul, don't frighten the life out of us.'

'Pádraig Keane came home from Dingle last night bringing only a stone of oatmeal and I'm sure that won't take him far.'

'Oh, that God in His mercy may not send any evil scourge down on Christians!'

'Amen,' said my father, and he went off about his business.

On the day the postman used to cross over to Dunquin in his currach we would all be waiting on the quay before him when he came in. He was always very soft with us. He used to open out the postbag to try and satisfy us. It was often he wasn't too thankful to us, all the same, for we used to be crowding in on top of the poor man. He wore a pair of spectacles and of course we thought it was queer to see spectacles on a man at that time. He was a hearty man that never left a person on the quay behind him, inside or outside the Island.

'Have you any news for us today, Pats?' Seán Fada asked him one day. 'How's the war going, or is any side giving in?'

'On my word, Seán, neither side is giving in yet, whatever. There's a paper inside here in the postbag and 'twould put the heart crossways in anyone who reads it. All that's in the world entirely now, Seán, is only slaughtering and battering and no one can say when there will be an end to it.'

'Yerra, leave them to it,' said Seán. 'We're far from them.'

'By my palms, Seán, I'm afraid there's trouble ahead for us such as there never was.'

'You must have good cause for saying it, man.'

'I have, Seán. I have letters here today under seal from Dublin Castle from England's man in Ireland, for the young lads of the Island, to tell them to be making themselves ready to go to the war. And isn't that bad news, man.'

'It isn't good or fit news,' said Seán, 'If only there was a remedy for it!'

There was squabbling there the likes of which no one had ever seen, for no one would take those letters from him, and he had to put them away again in his bag.

Your man went off up the boreen and he wasn't too well pleased with himself, for he had a letter for his own son as well as the next and that was the letter that he had no wish to hand over.

'Almighty God!' said Nell Mhór to my mother that evening. 'Isn't it the bad news we had today.'

'It is bad, my dear. We never knew misfortune rightly till this. You might easily know that the war wouldn't pass without having a poke at us.'

'What will our boys do now, Peig? I suppose they've no way out of it this turn, whatever.'

'Yerra, woman, "God is stronger than hope." Maybe that tyrant in Dublin Castle will have gone the Way of Truth before that horrid law is put into the practice.'

'Maybe so with God's help, Peig, and believe me, there would be no one lonesome after him. Sure, I'd say, Peig, that England would have enough men to gather into the army without coming to this Island looking for them.'

''Tis fine and soft you want it, Nell. Wouldn't they fill a gap in the field of battle as well as anyone else. This is the world, woman of my heart, where the men are needed.'

'God bless my soul, O Lord, if I have to be parted from Seáinín, Peig, I suppose 'tis in the madhouse I'll be found. I was heartbroken beyond anything when Máirín was swept away from me. But the memory of her has gone from me now. It was great ease to my mind to know that she was in

God's kingdom, a little angel without stain. But I tell you this firmly, if Seáinín goes from me, I won't survive at all.'

'I daresay, my poor woman. I'll have to part with Muiris too. The age that was in that notice is cleared by him with a month. God help us, isn't it for poor mothers that life is hard.'

'My love, my Lord God! Peig, isn't it true for you. Wasn't it little thought I had when I married Micil behind here that all this misfortune would be on top of me.'

'There was nothing troubling you that day, woman, only to be married to Micil.'

'There wasn't, Peig. I'd go anywhere by his side.'

'You would, my dear, and it is a stepmother that would blame you for it. We were all that way in our young days. But we had no cause for complaint till now. That God may help us!'

'Amen,' said Nell and they walked out side by side.

CHAPTER 12

Sitting on the Bank of the Strand

EVERYTHING shines very pleasantly for the person who has the youth and the health. They're the pair of precious jewels. But, my grief, they don't stay with a man always. They are little jewels that no one can keep a grip on.

There wasn't a thing in the world bothering me when I sat down on the bank of White Strand one lovely autumn evening. I was gazing out over the sea that was full of the birds of the ocean. My father and mother were in the field beside me binding oats. I wasn't long sitting on that grassy perch under the sun that was shining down when I started reflecting.

That was no wonder, for it was the lovely view from Gob Point across south to Iveragh and from there north to Brandon Creek. The golden mountains of Ireland were nodding their royal foreheads at me behind each other. It was they that had the fine, majestic appearance under their fleece of heather, though one could say that they should have lost their majesty long ago. A start was knocked out of me when someone spoke behind me.

'Isn't it as well for us to be making for home, my son?'

My father it was, coming up to call me.

'I suppose 'tis, Dad.'

''Tis, son. The dew is falling now and you've no business sitting on the grass after the sweat of the day. What was it you were gazing at?'

'I was gazing at those big mountains beyond and on the sea and the grand loveliness all around me.'

'Oh, the loveliness is there, pet. The stillness doesn't come properly on the sea till autumn. That's the time when the sea becomes dead calm and another thing, son, everything looks very beautiful when the stillness is there.'

'It seems so,' said I, rising. 'Look, the sea is like new milk and little silver bubbles on top of it, shining under the sun.'

'That's no wonder, for 'tis long since I saw a lovelier evening, praise and thanks be to God.'

When myself and my father came home, my mother had the supper ready. We had barely started eating when Diarmaid Thomáis rambled in. Himself and my father began to chat.

'Did ye finish at the oats yet, Patsy?' he said.

'We did,' said my father. ''Twas grand and dry today, man. It would only delight you to be dealing with it.'

''Tis the same story with everything you have a mind to do.'

'Faith, man, 'tis all one to me now, once 'tis off my hands.'

'I daresay it is only a worry to a man so long as it would be in swathes, but you got the weather the way you wanted it in the heel of the hunt.'

'I did, boy, great is the reward of patience.'

'Now, Patsy, let us leave that aside. Did you see those notices at all that came from Dublin Castle lately?'

'I did, and I curse them far from me! My son Muiris here has got one. The poor lad isn't happy in his mind ever since. His bit of food itself isn't doing him any good. I'm telling you, Diarmaid, it would be the happy day for us if that same Great War was over.'

'I'm telling you, Patsy, there's a broken heart in many a quarter over this war.'

'On my soul, 'tis no lie that there's many a woman and good man that had the nice comfortable life of it who're now left cold and hungry by it.'

'Some of the lads are thinking of lifting their wings and making for America.'

'I suppose that's only going from heat to cold for them, Diarmaid. When will they be off?'

'I couldn't tell you that, Patsy, but my own son is waiting to go and, since I'm telling it to a relation, I won't live after him from lonesomeness; I was very fond of him.'

'Wisha, my poor man, that's no wonder. Everyone is fond of his own. But maybe with God's help, Diarmaid, there might be peace soon and they wouldn't have to go away so quickly.'

'It would be a fine thing if there was, Patsy. They'd stay another while with us. 'Tis too long we'll be on our own.'

'Don't mind that, Diarmaid. You're a brave strong man still and if God leaves you life and health you'll be able to do your own work for a long while yet.'

'Wisha, from now on all that's in me is a very old soldier who has one leg in the grave and another on the edge. It won't be long now before my battle in this life is over, despite the best I can do. But I'd die happy if my son was settled down in America among his friends. I'm afraid, Patsy, that there's truth in the rumour going round about a warship that's to come to the Island.'

'Yerra, don't believe them, Diarmaid. Many stories fly about in time of war and no one should pay them any heed whatever.'

'You're right, Patsy. Certain people never stop making up stories and, on my oath, there isn't much sense to a deal of them. But, Patsy, you'd never tell me that it was time for me to go home.'

'You're not over the mark yet. The moon is hidden away now, but it will be a lovely night when she rises up.'

'Good-night now to ye,' said Diarmaid. 'I may as well be stirring myself.'

'Good luck to you, Diarmaid,' said my mother. 'We never felt the time passing. There's nothing like the company.'

CHAPTER 13

How the Warship came to the Island

IT was no great sleep I had that night, only thinking about the conversation between Diarmaid and my father. I knew well it was not without good reason that Diarmaid was so concerned over his son waiting to go to America. I knew my father was troubled in the same way, because my brother Muiris was waiting to go too. But he let on nothing.

What woke me in the morning was all the row and beating of hands outside the house. I leapt up and shoved my head out the window to see what was going on. What I saw was all the people running down to the quay.

'God of Miracles!' said I to my mother, 'what's up with the people that they're running down, or has someone from the village fallen down a cliff that they're making such a fuss?'

'No, child. Don't you see the warship?'

'Where is it?'

'Coming from North of Fiach, son. Diarmaid Thomáis was right last night when he said it was coming. All the boys have gone on the run back to Inish-vickillaun.'

When I put my head out the door again, the warship was riding at anchor and a small boat floating beside it with two sailors wearing white caps.

'Lord save us, they're landing,' said I.

'Leave them to it, son. The job's done now, thanks be to God. The lads have taken their legs clean away. The last currach has passed the Gob south with half an hour.'

My father came in.

'I don't think the small boat will land at all,' he said, 'for there is a rough choppy sea at the slip. The sailors were calling to us and what we understood from them was that they were short of fresh water.'

'That's better itself than any other bad thing,' said my mother. 'We're half out of our minds with the same hurly-burly. Eat your food, son, and don't mind them. Let them be coming in and out till they're tired of it.'

Nell Mhór dropped in and she was in a state.

'Great God, Peig Sayers, the likes of this day never came on top of me since I was baptized at the holy water font. I was racing round like a complete fool getting things ready for the poor boys who were heading for Inish-vickillaun this morning. They were in such a rush when they saw the warship coming from the North past Ferriter's Chase. Outside in the yard Seáinín was, and he pulling on his boots. Himself and Micil were up all last night. The black cow was calving and they had to stay with her till morning.'

'Did she calve?' my mother asked.

'She did this morning. A big bull calf she had.'

'Well,' said my father, 'someone will have to go up the hill and light a fire. No doubt the boys will be on the look-out for some signals from this place when the hunt will be over.'

'That would be a good plan,' said Nell. 'There's no need to let the lads settle themselves down for the night on a bleak island like Inish-vickillaun. Will there be anyone with you?'

'There will. A drove of us will be going there, for we'll have to bring a deal of turf with us to make a good fire.'

'You should take a drop of oil with you, so,' said my mother.

'A small drop of it would be a big help to us.'

''Tis here below beside the dresser, in a bottle all ready. Just pick it up.'

'All right, so. I'll be off. I daresay the other men are waiting for me.'

'If they are, you shouldn't be keeping them, but may

God bring ye safe, whatever.'

Out he went.

It was well dark when the boys came home, for they waited in Inish-vickillaun until the warship lifted anchor in White Strand bay and moved off Bray Head west. I'm telling you it was many the person that prayed from his heart that it wouldn't turn back to this place ever again.

CHAPTER 14

The Coming of Dónall O'Sullivan

ONE Sunday afternoon we were below on the strand playing football. There was no one in the village but was there, for they had no place else to gather after Mass. Dónall Mór O'Sullivan the old soldier, was amongst the crowd.

'*By Gor*,' said he, for that was a saying of his, 'there's life in the boys, God bless them.'

'On my word, they're tackling one another as hard as if there was a big bet on down there,' said Muiris Eoin Bháin.

'*By Gor*, the match will be fierce, Muiris.'

'They're all set for it,' said Muiris, answering him.

When the match was over Dónall O'Sullivan told us that he would start teaching us drill on Monday morning. We had a restless evening of it. Everyone was bursting to be a soldier. What else would satisfy the heart of a young man who was willing, but to be a soldier in the army of his own country? Dark Rosaleen was calling to her children to lift the slavery from her. We had all read the history of Ireland and we knew about the foul deeds of the English in our country, the way they used to torment and harass our ancestors. We would have the chance now to pay back the debt we owed to the enemy who was down on us.

Dónall O'Sullivan had come to teach us drill on Monday morning. We would be trained soldiers inside a month, to stand on the field of battle, if the call came. There was hustle and bustle among the boys throughout the evening. They talked about nothing else, hardly, except this new drilling. We could scarcely wait for the next morning to make a start, but we had to quieten ourselves down and wait patiently until Monday came.

But, my sharp grief, drilling was no easy work. It was many the curse I gave under my breath on the man that first invented it for a craft, but once I had learned it, it was great ease to my mind.

CHAPTER 15

The Rising

THREE days after Dónall left us, the terrible news came to us that Dublin City was burning down and that a big Rising was taking place there. We never expected that the fight would be on so soon. We thought it wouldn't start until Sir Roger Casement landed with arms. But it was how Casement had been caught by the British Army and taken across to England, and the arms in his care had been dumped to the bottom of the sea. We were bewildered. Where would we get guns? The guns had been promised us and we were planning to use them when the call came. But, sad to say, the driver that was making his way from Dublin to give us the call didn't succeed. An accident happened to him and he went astray. That left the people of Kerry in the dark about many things that were badly needed at the time. If he had succeeded in arriving safe, I suppose we would have a different story today. But the thing a man thinks worse than death may turn out to be his highest good.

'God bless my soul, Nell,' said my mother to Nell Mhór when she heard that the fight was on in Dublin, 'isn't there sound stuff in the Irishman?'

'Yerra, let me alone, woman of my heart, there's out and out war in the world altogether now.'

'There is, Nell, and it'll get worse I suppose, God help us. Don't you see that the war is gong on in our country now.'

'I hear there's some fighting going on in Dublin, I wonder if it's true?'

'It is true, Nell,' said my father. 'There is a Rising there with a couple of days. It is out and out war between the Irish and the English now and there's no knowing when 'twill end.'

'I wonder', asked my mother, 'will the Volunteers from hereabouts go up to Dublin?'

'I don't think they will,' said my father. 'They didn't get the order to go.'

'I wonder why not?'

'I suppose the officers in charge of the Rising didn't want to send for them, because Casement was arrested and the ship with the arms had sunk to the bottom of the sea.'

'The boys won't go off to the fight so, Patsy,' said Nell.

'I don't think they'll go this turn, whatever, Nell, but they won't be idle by and by for, my dear woman, the fight has only started now. That flag that Pearse raised in the royal capital of Ireland won't ever again be lowered. For I'm telling you, woman, every mother's son in the country is true to that flag.'

'No wonder they would be,' said Nell. 'It is a noble flag. There's something about it that would make you have love for it and the people that are waving it.'

'You're right, Nell' said my father. 'There's no place where you'd see that flag that you wouldn't feel glad in your heart over it.'

'The enemy hate it like poison,' said my mother.

'No wonder they would,' said my father, 'for 'tis often the men that were true to that flag destroyed and scattered them and they'll destroy and scatter them now, too, with God's help.'

'Yourself saying it and God answering you, Patsy,' said Nell, 'and for a surety it wouldn't knock any stir out of our hearts if we saw that same enemy drowned out there in the bay.'

With that she left.

A couple of days later the postman was out in the main-

land and everybody's heart was high that there would be
good news.

When he landed back Seán Fada asked if he had any news.

'On my soul, Seán, I have no good news today, whatever.
The Rising that was in Dublin is over since yesterday morn-
ing. The leaders – no but the chieftains I should say – of the
Volunteers are arrested and have been sent over to England.
The Army shot the biggest part of them. Patrick Pearse has
fallen.'

'Is he dead?'

'He is, Seán, and his brother was executed too and many
gentlemen besides. There is terror in the hearts of everyone in
the whole country today. The terrible destruction brought on
the people in Dublin by the English finished the Rising. But I
think myself that the English will pay dearly for it yet, for
instead of the Irish losing heart, it only gave them more courage. I never before saw the people so stirred.'

'I suppose, Pats,' said my father, 'that they're no omen of
peace for England?'

'They're not, Patsy. The old hatred that was ever there
between Ireland and England is as fresh today before the
minds of the people as it was hundreds of years ago. Unless
I'm greatly mistaken, the fight will soon be on all over Ireland.'

'God save us, I suppose it will,' said my father. 'They're set
upon it, it seems.'

'On my soul, men,' said Seán Fada, 'it's no good for us to
run away or to find a leafy shade. If 'tis in store for us to fall
on the battlefield, isn't it said to us by the leaders of our
Faith that a man can't have a more glorious death than to die
for his country.'

'You're right, Seán,' said my father, 'but all the same that
wouldn't stop a man being afraid.'

'Yerra, man, wasn't it little fear the heroes had who rose

out against the red arms of England in Dublin this week past,' said Seán.

'They were a class of men, Seán,' said my father, 'and may God have mercy on them, that had their minds made up for this work. They preferred to die than to see Dark Rosaleen in slavery.'

'She is the costly Dark Rosaleen to them,' said Seán. 'It is many the good man that fell during the week for her.'

'On my soul, but more will fall for her sake,' said my father.

'I'm afraid, Patsy,' said the postman, 'the number of men that fell in Easter Week won't be the last in this country, before there's an end of it.'

With that he went off up the boreen.

The postman was right, for it wasn't long before the fight started in earnest throughout the whole of Ireland.

CHAPTER 16

My Term at School finished

MY term at school was over by this time and since my father had no money to spend on me, I had to stay at home and cast aside the wish I had to go to the College.[1] I took up fishing in earnest, a trade I seldom boasted about afterwards.

Tomás and Eibhlín were going to school yet for they were younger than me, but my two other brothers, Pádraig and Muiris, and my sister Cáit, were grown up at this time and making out for themselves. Cáit was in service with a school-master in Limerick. Father O'Mahony it was that took her in hand. My mother had no hesitation therefore in letting her hit for the road with the priest. She had a good guardian. Pádraig and Muiris were fishing and doing fine. It was high time for me too to be looking out for myself from now on.

The big Races were to be held in Ballintagart and all the lads were going there, but I had no pennies in my own pocket unless my father gave them to me and, on my oath, they weren't too plentiful by him at this time. I didn't know how to come by a couple of shillings that would see me through the Races but, as luck would have it, a couple of days before a pair of gentlemen came to the Island. They strolled back to White Strand and called the lads to go with them. We went eagerly and pointed out the boreen to the strand. They were very thankful to us and asked if we'd like to have a little race. Páidín Mhuiris said we would if they started it off.

'I'll give half a crown to the winner of the race and a shilling to the lad who comes in second,' said one of the strangers. 'Are ye satisfied?'

[1] i.e. Secondary school.

'We are, sir,' said Páidin.

Yerra, reader, my heart was pounding inside me with
eagerness to run so long as I'd have pennies for Ballintagart
Races. I said to myself that I'd find out if my body and legs
had it in them.

There was no one in the bunch I was more afraid of than
Tom Eoin Bháin, for he was a stocky, well-built, strong lad
and he had great speed. It was often before I had trial of him
and he always won, but of course I never exerted myself to
the utmost any time I raced against him until now. I was set
on not letting him win that day, whatever.

One of the strangers went to the head of the strand and
stood there.

'Now then,' said the other man, 'I'll give ye handicaps, for
some of ye are younger than the others and it wouldn't be
right to be unfair to anyone.'

We were still hopping around in a scramble making a hul-
labaloo, but the stranger lined us all up, everyone on his
own mark according to age. It happened that myself and
Tom Eoin Bháin were arranged shoulder to shoulder in the
last line. The rest of the lads were well out in front. I looked
at Tom. His face was pure white.

'Have no fear,' said I, 'if we're beaten itself it will be no
shame to us. Look at the distance the rest are out in front.'

'I don't care,' said he, 'I'll do my best,' and he turned
away without another word. The stranger moved a little
away and pulled a white handkerchief out of his pocket. He
raised the handkerchief and we were off.

Soon I heard someone shouting 'Let go!' One lad had trip-
ped up another beside me, but I didn't stop. My great long
nose was cutting the wind in front of me and my two eyes
were glued on the man standing at the head of the strand.
The distance between me and him was shortening rapidly.
But beside me were two others who were running level with
me, Tom Eoin Bháin and Páidín Mhuiris. There was nothing

between the three of us when we reached the man at the head
of the strand. It was together we took the turn round him.
The rest of the lads were chasing us furiously. Tomáisín Carney and Muiris Mháire Eoin were at our heels. Any one of us
in front would only have to make the slightest stumble and
they would be well out ahead.

The mad scramble and helter-skelter was on, reader, as we
tried to best each other. In the gallop Tom Eoin Bháin and
Páidín Mhuiris bumped into one another and straight away
the pair of them were rolling over together on the strand. Of
course that suited me for I was gasping for breath and the
sweat blinding me at the time. It was myself that was thankful when the gentleman handed me my stump of a half-
crown. Tomáisín Carney got a shilling and Muiris Mháire
Eoin Bháin sixpence. I had the money for the Races without
thanks to anyone and I'm telling you I knocked sport out of
the day.

There was a band of us together going to Dingle on the day
of the Races. We were up Classach Hill when Seáinín the
'Fuss' from Cam joined us.

'Is it to the Races you're going, Seáinín?' asked Seán Fada.

''Tis, my dear man. Isn't it many the day we'll spend in
the clay, sure?'

'True for you,' said Seán Fada, 'and God help us, there
won't be many thinking of us, I suppose.'

Oyeh, sweet man, let them be. It would do us little good
for them to be thinking of us. We must spend a day like this
always, so long as we have the strength.'

A tough, hard man Seáinín was and good company too.
Himself and Seán Fada were chatting away and we never felt
the journey over Classach Hill, for good as Seáinín was, Seán
Fada was a better man for the crack. Their voices never stop-
ped from the time we left Classach Top until we reached
Dingle. Seáinín used to mix twenty stories into one. Seán
Fada said he'd stand him a pint of porter when we reached

Dingle, if he sang a song for us.

'Wisha, may God not impoverish your hand,' he said. 'I'll sing a song, too, for ye and welcome and 'tisn't because of the drink but because I like to be in yeer company.'

He then struck up 'The Sailorman', and you'd go anywhere to listen to him, for the afternoon was lovely and a perfect stillness there. Seáinín had the voice of the fairies, if ever a man had it. When the song was finished all of us clapped him.

'Long life to you, Seáinín,' said Seán Fada. 'On my word, you've the drink well earned and we mustn't back out of it when we reach Dingle.'

Seán Fada didn't break his promise when we landed. He caught Seáinín by the shoulders and took him off to O'Shea's public house. The rest of the Island people followed them inside and they had a drink together.

We took a rest for ourselves that evening and stayed in Máirtín Keane's public house till morning. It was too late to go out to the racecourse by the time we had a bite of food eaten and the dust of the road cleaned from our clothes. At daybreak next morning we were up. As early as it was, Máirtín was up before us, and his daughter Máire. They were going to the Races themselves too. She had the breakfast ready on the table; all we had to do was sit down and eat it. The whole company sat round the table. More and more country people were crowding into the kitchen until it was how the house was bursting with them. The noise and din started.

'Men, said Seán Fada, 'haven't ye any manners at all, to be crowding into the place where the poor people out from the Island are eating? Shove back, please, and let them eat a bite. Maybe these poor men won't get a chance to put another bite in their mouths until next day again.'

'True for you, man of my heart,' said Máirtín, but these country caubogues don't care so long as they're fine themselves.'

An Island house in ruins: 'All I can see today are the old ruined houses where people used to live.'

Soon the people of the Island had plenty of room, for as soon as the others had a couple of jorums taken they moved off to the racecourse.

Shortly afterwards we followed them out. When we reached the racecourse there wasn't the width of my palm of it that wasn't black with people. There were tents and platforms here and there in the field and throngs of people gathered round them. The people running the sideshows were doing well, for it is around them the crowds flocked. Seán Fada called his own people into the tent where drink was for sale. Myself and Tom Eoin Bháin and Páidín Mhuiris went off around the field. We stopped now and then, looking at the sideshows.

'Faith, Tom,' said I, 'isn't it great to be at the Races.'

'It is,' he said. 'The greed for sweets and cakes has been knocked out of me today. Come on up here, there's a crowd gathered. There must be something strange going on.'

'We might as well,' said Páidín. 'The horses will be galloping soon. Look, they're putting them under starter's orders already.'

When we went where the crowd was gathered, there was a small sallow man with a stoop on him in the middle of them and you'd hear him back at Buncala. He was reading fortunes for anyone that wanted it. Soon I saw a middle-aged legger of a man pushing his way through to him. He made no stop until he was beside the sallow man, who jumped up as soon as he saw him.

'By heaven, a thousand welcomes to you, Seán.'

'Life and health to yourself,' Seán replied. 'I had little thought when I left the Island yesterday afternoon that we'd meet together here.'

'Oh, the people meet one another, boy.'

'It looks like it,' Seán said. 'Come on and we'll have a drink. Maybe we won't meet at any races ever again.'

'Maybe so, and since we're here, a small drop of drink won't kill us.'

'Faith, Tom,' said I to Tom Eoin Bháin, 'everybody knows Seán Fada.'

'They do, boy,' said Tom. 'The head princes know one another.'

Soon afterwards the race started – eight horses in the first race and it was no lie to call them horses. They were smooth and groomed with a shine on their pelts. The betting men weren't idle; they were making enough rumpus. It wouldn't be any wonder if they got hoarse from bawling. My head was splitting from the din.

Myself and Tom Eoin Bháin and Páidín Mhuiris went off to a spot where we had a good view of the horses. Soon they were off and all the people around the tents turned to look at them. They were a lovely sight, eight good horses and his own jockey proudly riding each one. They went round well the first time but, when they were finishing the course the second time, one of the two front horses stumbled and the jockey was pitched headlong to the ground. The horse dragged him along. Everyone thought he was killed, but no. The people gathered round and he was taken off to the hospital. Everyone looking at the race said he had every chance of winning that day, if the horse hadn't stumbled.

When myself and Tom Eoin Bháin and Páidín Mhuiris came back to the tents, Seán Fada was in great fettle, himself and Seáinín the 'Fuss' from Cam and the sallow man. He had a hold of Seáinín by the hand and the sallow man held the other while he was singing a song. Not many stayed on the racecourse when they heard the singing. They all gathered round them.

There was another race after that, but it wasn't as good as the first, nor were the horses as sleek. The time was slipping away and we were getting tired of traipsing around all day. I called Tom Eoin Bháin and Páidín Mhuiris and we left the racecourse. Several people were leaving at the same time. We strolled in along the road until we came to Máirtín Keane's. The rest of the Island people were following on. We weren't long inside when they landed. There was no chance they would turn for home without paying a visit to Máirtín's public house, for it was there the Races would end.

A good man in a tight corner was Máirtín. He would never leave any of the Islanders out under the sky of the night when he came across them. He used to have the bright welcome for them always. Signs on, they all wanted to go to Máirtín's at the time of a Races and make a day of it. It was almost night when we set off on the long road home.

It isn't because I say it, but there was a grand bunch of men and fine graceful girls coming out of the Island at that time, though it would be easy for us to deny it today. Some of us were airy enough. For that reason the long road before us didn't cost us a thought.

As soon as we came home my mother welcomed us. But my father didn't stay to say 'God bless' in the door itself. He had to go to drive back the cow that was on the mountain, west at the Top of Two Glens. She had stayed behind there grazing after the rest and there was no hurry home on her, for the night was grand and soft. My father preferred to spend a while walking than to sit inside. He had his own reason for that. The grand fragrant air of the night would take away the smell of the drink from him and my mother wouldn't be going on about the spree he was after having. He had a little drop taken. Why wouldn't he, it isn't always a poor man has a chance to go in the company of his friends.

'I suppose', my mother said, 'you've plenty of news from the Races.'

'On my oath I have,' said I, and I started telling her about all I'd seen.

'God bless my soul, the Ballintagart Races were great out this year.'

'I heard they weren't so good for many a long day.'

'They weren't, child. I remember well a time when there were no Races there. It was on Ventry Strand the Races used to be held. But every life is changing. Where did the rest stay behind you?'

'Muiris and a crowd more were following on behind us,' I said.

'He took a drop?'

'Everyone else took a drop as well as him but there was no one drunk.'

'That's good, child. The drink is ruin.'

I didn't wait for the rest to come back from the Races. I was dropping off to sleep beside the fire. It stole on me in the end and I stayed there without a stir out of me until the sun rose next morning.

CHAPTER 17

How the Volunteer came on the run to the Island

THE sun was high over Mount Eagle when I rose. I had a lame man's step, for my boot had been pinching me on my way home from the Races the day before. When I had the breakfast eaten, my mother told me to go down the White Strand Field to mind the cow. Whatever gaping round I was having as I stood at the door, I saw a couple of men running east to the quay.

'There's something up, Mom,' said I.

'Is it anything you see?'

''Tis, Mom. There's a couple of men running the road east. There's something strange going on at the bottom of the village.'

'That would be no wonder, child. The British soldiers are very busy at this present time. Maybe 'tis some of them that have come to the Island.'

'Maybe so,' said I, and I didn't wait to say another word, but off out with me.

Who would be coming against me the road west but Nell Mhór, and she running.

'Faith,' says I, 'I won't have to go another step. It's to my mother Nell's coming and she has the story in her gob.'

I came back. I was barely inside when Nell was in at my heels.

'God save you here, Nell,' said my mother. 'It is to you the news comes.'

'Long life to ye, Peig. It seems you never heard a scrap.'

'The devil a thing, woman. What's the story you have now?'

'Well, Peig, one of the Volunteers has come to the Island on the run.'

'I suppose it was to meet him the people were running down the road east a while ago?'

'It was, my dear. He landed unknown to us nearly. The poor boy is very much afraid that the hunt will be after him.'

'There was a battle there so?'

'There was, woman, and a bloody battle.'

'Where, Nell?'

'I heard it was at Lispole they were at grips with one another and that the road is red with blood from there to Dingle.'

'That won't do, woman, but begin at the start of your story and tell it to me properly,' said my mother.

'I give you my word, Peig dear, I was no hand ever at telling a story in proper order. But this is how I heard it myself, word for word. Between Dingle and Lispole, at the side of the road, there was an old schoolhouse. In that old schoolhouse the Volunteers were gathered. They were going to attack the British Army when they came that way. They had the place well secure and a look-out posted, from whichever direction the enemy would come. They were ready for them, but God help us, the enemy came and the boys were beaten in the battle. But all the same they fought on till the schoolhouse was burned on top of them. That was when they gave in to the enemy. Some of them were taken prisoner, but more of them managed to escape. The boy who came on the run to the Island today had been caught by the enemy. A British officer was escorting him down across the field to his motor car, when he spotted one of the Volunteers lying in wait in a nook in the ditch and his gun aimed at him. The British officer was trembling hand and foot when he saw him and he let the two prisoners he had go. When the Volunteer saw what the officer had done, he never fired any shot at him.'

'It was well he did that,' said my mother. 'Good never

went astray on anyone. But how did they get on after, Nell?'

'When they were driven out of the schoolhouse they scattered east and west. Everyone was making out for himself from then on. The enemy slipped away down-hearted into their motor cars and headed for Dingle, but all the length of the road there were red bullets being fired at them. The amount of blood on the road this morning was frightful. 'Tis said that many of the British soldiers who landed in Dingle that night are dead.'

'That was no wonder, Nell. The battle was hot there, it seems.'

'It was, Peig, and all the roads are trenched. They say that no horse and cart can go Pollgorm east. The roads are trenched in three places and the wonder with everyone is where was the clay put that was in the trenches.'

'The boys aren't idle, Nell, that God may strengthen them. That's a great drawback to the enemy, not to be allowed to travel in their motor cars from place to place.'

'It is surely, Peig, but all the same it is the poor Irish I dare say who will pay for this work in the heel of the hunt, for the power that's against us is too strong.'

'Don't mind that, Nell, don't you know that a good true soldier is better in his own country than twenty useless sprassauns.'

'If it were God's will, Peig, that there might be an end to the war without harm or damage to us, we'd have the peace of God again.'

'On my word, Nell, it will take another while before it is finished.'

'I dare say, Peig. We've no business letting our feathers droop.'

'You'd stay talking for ever, Nell,' said I, 'and I'd stay listening to you. Ye're the amazing pair for gabbing, yourself and my mother here. The both of ye have the gift for it.'

I left them there and went off to herd the cow.

CHAPTER 18

The British Soldier on Ballymullen Bridge and how he let the Islandman go ahead

A WEEK after this there was a British soldier standing on Ballymullen Bridge, his gun in his hand, and he wouldn't let a man or woman go into Dingle. The people were in a bad way, but what could they do? No one had courage enough to go near him. If he did, he would be the man that wouldn't come back, maybe, for the British soldiers were very disturbed over their losses in the battle of Lispole. He had a bad reputation, too, beyond all the other soldiers in Dingle. It was said that he had burned down a whole town, because there had been a bloody battle a little way from that town and the officer in command had been killed. It was said, too, that some of the soldiers had been trying to stop him from doing this terrible harm, but he wouldn't give in to them.

The road was black with people this day and no matter what they did, neither a man nor a woman would be let into the big town of Dingle. A man from the Island was amongst the throng.

'I'd say, wisha,' said he, 'if I was allowed to go and talk to that man he would let me into Dingle to do my messages.'

It was how the rest were mocking him, saying that it was high notions the likes of him had, a man from the Island beyond. But a big caubogue of a farmer down from Ballycote spoke out.

'Let him go,' said he, 'since he's so foolish. It won't be long till the man of the shouting beyond gives him a different story, for that is what he wants surely, otherwise he wouldn't be so eager as all that, though we're sorry to see him meeting his downfall on this ground here today when we're not able to rescue him. But 'tis ever said, men, that there's no accounting for taste. Leave him to it.'

'On my soul, it isn't my death at the hands of that little raspín of a British soldier beyond that's the worse for ye, men,' said the Islandman, and his anger blazed. 'It is a bad name ye'll have in the lore of the Irish ever and always. It will be thrown at ye, and yeer stock after ye, that there's one small soldier from the land of the enemy standing on this bridge today keeping ye from stirring since morning. I'd prefer a bullet through my body in the world that's in it today, bad as it might be, rather than to give it to say to anyone that would come after me that that little raspín of a soldier could stop me from going into Dingle to do my messages.'

'It is the bullet that'll be sent through your body, you poor man,' said a well-spoken old woman who was sitting in an ass's cart.

'If it is itself, good woman, aren't there better men than me lying still in death from the bullets already.'

'You're right, I suppose,' she said. 'It is the lack of courage that's on us.'

The Islandman pushed his way through the crowd until he was in front of the soldier.

'Stop! said the soldier angrily. The Islandman stopped and gave a woebegone look at the soldier.

'Where are you going?'

'I'm going to Dingle, sir.'

'Where are you from?' said the soldier, aiming his gun.

'From the West, from the Island, wisha, sir, the furthest point west in Ireland.'

'Oh, I understand; they're honest people in that place who don't bother anybody. In with you to Dingle, in spite of these here, Islandman. Do your messages there and take all the time you want for it.'

The Islandman went into Dingle and his heart as light as a blackbird's.

No other man or woman was let into Dingle that day and the country people had to go home heavy-hearted.

There was wonder and amazement over what trick the Islandman had played on the British soldier, that he let him go into Dingle before the eyes of all the men and women there, but they never found it out. When the Islandman had done his messages in Dingle he came home and no one frowned at him.

The country people were in a tight fix at that time, but those who lived close to Dingle, and had the opportunity, used to take away whatever they needed across the hill during the night, secretly. But praise and thanks be to God, shortly afterwards everyone was allowed into Dingle, the same as always.

CHAPTER 19

How Cáit came home from Limerick and how we scattered from one another

WHEN my father came home from fishing, I heard him telling my mother that he ought to be in Dingle for the Saturday, since my sister Cáit was coming home from Limerick and she would have to have someone there to meet her.

'By the Lord, you're right,' said my mother. 'You could do worse than go, if the day is fine.'

My heart jumped for joy when I heard my sister Cáit was coming. It was more than two years since she was last home, so I had a welcome in my heart for Cáitín.

A couple of days passed and on Saturday, at the fall of night, in the door she landed, a fine strapping woman. My mother gave her a loving kiss, no wonder, and took the great coat she wore to hang on a nail.

There was no telling the fine stories she had about her travels. She let my father know that she was finished with Limerick.

'What makes you say that, weren't you in a good house?' said my father.

'I had no fault with the people of the house. I was very fond of my mistress, and so far as the man goes, he was like a father to me for the time I was there. But all the same I won't go to Limerick in service ever again.'

'All right so, girl,' said my father. 'A person's life is his own,' and out he went.

My brother Pádraig had by this time grown into a big strong man. He had no wish for the Island and off he went to America when he got the passage money from my Aunt Kate. I think he wouldn't have gone so early but for the acci-

dent that happened to our brother, poor Tomás.[1] From the
day Tomás died he started to lose interest in the work of
house and place. He was like a man half asleep and half
awake.

'I couldn't live with the lonesomeness here,' he said to my
mother. 'I was very fond of Tomás, but now, since he died, I
won't cross over the hill-top of the Island ever again.'

'Well and good, son,' said my mother. 'You may as well be
doing something for yourself, so follow those that are going to
America. Muiris and Micheál will stay another while with
me, but I suppose it won't be long, may God help us.' She
turned up to the corner and started to cry.

A month from that day, Pádraig went to America. There
was a band of boys and girls from the Island with him. It was
the first drop downhill the Island got, for since then, according as a man is able to go, he's off, and soon there won't be
anybody living here.

Pádraig was in America only the two years when he sent the
passage money to my sister Cáit. Cáit had no wish to go, but
when she got the fare she didn't like to draw back. God helps
the weak, so she took heart and over she went. As soon as she
had a little money earned, she sent for her elder brother
Muiris, and off with him too across the sea.

Muiris found good work and it is often the pair of them
would visit my Aunt. She was proud of Cáit, for she was a
sensible girl who would take good advice from her Aunt.
She wasn't like many more of them round the place, who
preferred to have their own way, so my Aunt was very fond of
her.

My father was asleep in his grave among his friends when
Muiris left home. Muiris had no wish to go to America, any
more than Cáit, but what was there for him to do here? He
hadn't a penny nor a thing to show for his life, so when he

[1] Aged 21, he fell down a cliff while pulling heather for firing.

got the passage money from his sister he gathered his last and his awl and away he went.

Eight years Pádraig had spent in America when he got a longing to pay a visit home. He wrote to my mother saying that he would be back with her before long, that he wanted to see his own beautiful sun-village again, and especially his mother, the person he loved most in the world. My mother laughed and cried while she was reading that letter.

At this time my sister Eibhlín was in service in Dublin with a man of the O'Sheas in Dundrum and she liked it greatly to be there. She told us in a letter that the O'Sheas were very homely people and that she was a pet by them. That much was great consolation to my mother, for her family was the whole world to her always.

CHAPTER 20

How Páidraig came home from America and took my Sister Eibhlín back with him

WE were not expecting Pádraig when he walked in the door and, reader, he knocked a start out of us. He came at the beginning of February in 1928, when the Island was covered with snow. A cow or calf couldn't be let out to graze, the snow was so heavy.

Pádraig was only home from America a week, when he went to Dublin to visit Eibhlín. My mother had no notion at all that he would bring her back home with him until they landed in to us a couple of days after. She would have preferred it if Eibhlín stayed where she was, but Pádraig wouldn't be satisfied without bringing her back, and, when he was leaving home, he took her off with him to America. My mother was heart-broken, and no wonder, for so long as Eibhlín was in Dublin she could expect to see her some time, but the last sight she ever saw of her was the day when Pádraig took her away.

On the morning of the day he was leaving, he was standing at the door looking down onto the strand. Unknown to him, I was watching. He was standing still, deep in thought. He turned to me.

'Micheál,' he said, stretching his hand towards me. I took his hand and gripped it fondly. 'You'll be with us yet too, with God's help.' There was a sob in his voice.

'Wisha, brother of my heart, you did more harm than good to me coming to Ireland, for there is as much lonesomeness on me at this present time that it would kill the strongest man in the Island.'

'Don't mind that, boy,' said he, and the words were failing

him with the dint of his sorrow. 'Everything will turn out well yet.'

My mother was sitting in the corner crying. The memory of that day will stay in her head for ever, for despite all she had gone through in the past, she never got a harder blow than separating from Pádraig and Eibhlín. I followed them down to the quay myself.

'The blessing of God go with ye now,' said I. 'A safe journey to ye and may we see one another again in prosperity and good health.'

'Amen,' said Pádraig, stepping into the currach.

My mother was very worried until she got a letter from them, but from then on she began shaking herself up again.

CHAPTER 21

The great Change that came over the Minds of the People on the Island and how I went to America myself

THE year after Pádraig and Eibhlín went to America, a great change came over the minds of the people on the Island. None of them wanted to stay there. Even the old people preferred to be living on the mainland. The old men were dying, and the old women too, and there was no one coming, nor any hope of them, to fill the empty seats. My father and Diarmaid Thomáis and Seán Fada and the postman, and I could mention more, were gone to join the dead inside a couple of years and it was a great loss altogether to a small village for so many people to be gone from it in so short a time.

It was a drawback to me that Pádraig and Eibhlín were gone, for all I had to run the place with me was an old man,[1] not too strong, who was poor help at any task or job. My mother was getting well on in years and wasn't able to go to hill or mountain any more.

I was pulling away with me through life, with one day easy and another hard, until my brother Pádraig sent the passage money to me. I wasn't expecting it at all. Yerra, reader, it was myself that was in an awful fix. How could I leave my mother behind all on her own on an Island in the sea? If I could take her over with me to America it would be all right, but I had no way of doing that at the time. It was as much as I could do to manage it myself. Think of the hobble I was in, reader. I was going against God, surely, to leave her on her own on the Island without anyone to look after her. But at

[1]His uncle.

the same time, life was hard and I had nothing to do here. I thought in my own mind that if God spared me the health, I would gather a share of money and come home to my mother and we would have a pleasant, comfortable life together.

The morning I said goodbye and farewell to my mother, my two eyes were red from crying. But she told me to take heart, that God was powerful and had a good mother.

'Son of my heart,' she said, 'it is a poor place where you wouldn't be better off than here. Don't you see that everyone is running away from it if he can. You'll be amongst your own brothers, whatever life is in store for you. There will be people enough living from hand to mouth here. I don't want to wrong you any more than any of the others. Goodbye now, dear, and may God bring you safe.'

My mother was heart-broken altogether, but she kept it to herself so long as I was before her. I was very troubled until I reached Dingle, but I'm telling you, reader, that I met enough company there and it wasn't long until the lonesomeness lifted and I shook myself up. Three days later I was on board ship going to America and if I hadn't gay company it isn't day yet. There was a band of young men and graceful girls from every part of Ireland along with me. But it is myself that was shy amongst them since I had no English, only the odd word that was no use. I made bold with them in the end and soon we were fine and friendly enough together.

Luck was with me and I landed in America after spending eight days at sea. We had a good ship and the sea was smooth and calm, not a stir in any direction but like a pane of glass. I wasn't short of food or drink or anything else in the world and, as far as company goes, we had that too, so much so, reader, that it was too quickly the days went past me.

I wasn't long in America before I cursed myself for going there at all. I couldn't find any work and it was how I used to hang my head with shame to be going to my Aunt's house every afternoon. My thousand sorrows! It was then I re-

The author's mother

pented, but I didn't let on that anything was troubling me till I got the chance to come home. I left them then. Cáit was mad with me for saying I would do the like and Muiris and Pádraig were down on top of me for doing it. But if they gave me honey on plates, I wouldn't stay another day or night.

God was thankful to me, however, for I was home only a little while when a lady came to the Island, Máire Kennedy, who is noted for a long time among the Gaels of Ireland. She became acquainted with my mother and they grew to be close friends. Máire would never be satisfied at all until we started to write a book.[1] A year later the book was published by Talbot & Co. Ltd., Dublin, and there was great call for it. It was this book, along with God's help, that gave the first lift up to myself and my mother.

As I said before, God helps the weak, for the book was only on the market a month when I got sick and had to go into Dingle hospital for a while. I'll have to admit that a good nurse was looking after me. She was the kind Sister Patricia, may God reward her work. But for the gentle care I got from her, I suppose I wouldn't be alive today. I wasn't long in her hands when I was able to walk in and out for myself again. Soon after that I came home as well as ever.

[1] *Peig.*

CHAPTER 22

The Strangers on the Island

IN those days many strangers used to visit the Island from time to time. Amongst them was Doctor 'Blahín',[1] an easy-going man and a man with a big heart too. There wasn't a head of a house in the village that didn't receive a present of money from him when he would be going back home. He never came empty to us, may it bring him luck, and the amazing thing was that the man who was after coming over from the City of London hadn't the English cramp on his tongue. You couldn't say this about many of our own people who came to us from the cities of Ireland. Aristotle himself wouldn't understand them, though he was a learned man.

One evening I came home from fishing and Doctor 'Blahín' was inside before me. He had a big box at the head of the table and anyone would declare from all the fuss that there was something good inside it. No wonder my mother thought her fortune was made when she saw how elegant it was. She could hardly wait for 'Blahín' to get up and open the ornamental chest.

'Now, Peig,' said he at last, rising and opening it, 'I suppose you never before saw the likes of this talking machine. When I was here last, you used to be telling me grand stories beside the fire. It ran into my head then that if I had this machine, I could take all those stories away with me, so if I lived to come to the Blasket again, I would bring it. Would you mind at all putting one of the fine stories you have onto it?'

[1] Dr. Robin Flower, translator of *An t-Oileánach* (*The Islandman*). 'Blahín' is a diminutive of the Irish word for 'flower'.

'"Blahín,"' said my mother, 'all that's in me is a poor tormented woman, but I wouldn't mind if I thought the boys and girls of my own country would profit from my labours.'

'My hand and word to you,' said he, 'that's the way it will be.'

Then my mother started with her stories, and well able she was to tell them, even though I say it myself. But, by my palms, Doctor 'Blahín' never let her go thirsty, for he always gave her the drop of whiskey.

When his term on the Island was over and he was going home next day, or the day after, he called in to say goodbye to us. And if he did, it wasn't cold or empty he came.

'Now, Peig,' said he, 'I'm off home to my own country the first fine day I get.'

'Good luck to you, boy,' said my mother.

'Here's this little gift,' said he, handing her a five pound note.

My mother didn't want to take it from him, but it was no use arguing.

'Take it, Peig, it will keep you in the little bit of tobacco for a while.'

He said goodbye to us then and went away. It is my mother that was pleased to get the lump of money and many the blessing went from her heart to the man who gave it.

It was often strangers used to visit our house. We had a long, wide kitchen for them, where they were let dance and caper. My mother loved the company always and company was what the strangers wanted. They liked to come where they were welcome and wherever in the village they could get a fiddle, they brought it with them for the night.

Their shanks wouldn't be cold by the time the dance was finished, I'm telling you. Many the gay evening we spent like that until the strangers stopped visiting us. When they left us the girls of the Island had nothing to do. They had no wish to marry here, for they had seen enough of marriage among the older people.

At that time two girls from the Island married two of the strangers. O King of Miracles, what an upheaval there was in the village! I'm telling you, reader, that the girls spared neither the rouge nor the brilliantine. They would be eyeing one another to see which of them was done up the best. There was no chance anybody would catch one of the girls wearing the same clothes in the evening that she had on in the morning. She'd have a different outfit entirely. It was no good a girl having long stockings without short stockings to the ankle as well. But it isn't with fine clothes only that the men are won; there has to be more besides.

When they failed to make ground with the crowd with the white trousers, they lifted their wings and married farmers' sons over on the mainland who hadn't a stitch. There are some girls left on the Island yet, but I dare say they will copy the others, unless they're expecting more of the crowd with the white trousers to come their way. Their gamble will put off the day of reckoning, I suppose.

CHAPTER 23

I'm thinking sadly about the Life that is gone

THE world is a strange and lonesome place today compared to when I was growing up. I'm thinking about all the people that were there in my time, and have departed from this world for ever, may God grant rest in heaven to their souls.

It is sad my thoughts are when I look back on the gay life I've had. The long years have vanished and all I can see today are the old ruined houses where people used to live. I remember strong and brave men and women to be living in the houses that are, my sorrow, ruined now. Twelve houses have gone to rack, to my memory, that were at their height in my young days. Cliff grass and nettles are growing round them today.

Would it be any wonder for me to be sad, reader, that saw sport and company in those houses? It is many a boy and graceful girl in Ireland who has the opportunity to travel and see things more pleasant than I have here. All the same, I don't fault this lonesome spot, for I don't believe there is a corner in Ireland more beautiful. The sea and the rocks and the dark ravines and the mountains of Ireland are out there in front of me, with no mist over them. They are a fine sight on a day of sunshine. But they are finer again, when the winter's storm is there. The wind lifts the grey mist from their foreheads.

Neither cold nor frost nor rain cracks the mountains. They have the same noble shape to them always. If they are in the tight grip of the years itself, they show no signs of it, for they look as pleasing as they did ever. The same sweet smell rises from their heather. The little birds sing gaily on top of the rocks and the waves are for ever murmuring their lament in the dark caves.

But, my sharp bitter grief, our friends and relations will never come back again. The empty seats will never be filled; the lovely, gay music won't be played, the clattering of feet on the floor won't be heard, nor the sweet, singing laughter. In their place, wild birds are nesting in ruins that once were sweet to my heart. The people living in them were swept away out of this life. May God give us grace to live according to His true, holy will, for in this life altogether, there is only emptiness compared to the spiritual joy that God grants to those who put their entire faith and trust in Him. O God who is in heaven, O Holy Creator, grant us to taste Thy kingly sweetness in our hearts for, however long the day, the night is sure to come. The day of our death is in store for us too, may God grant us help to meet it.

I don't know what is laying bare thoughts so sad as these in my heart. They rush in without me searching for them. I drive them away, but here they are again in heavy, black showers.

I remember when this place was at its height and the fishing good but, God help us, that day is past and things have changed. There is neither spirit nor drive in the people today. They have no inclination for fishing either, even if the fish were there. There isn't a man today whose catch would compare with that of the old people. The old custom is at an end and I'm afraid that living on the Island is at an end too.

It is well I remember fine mornings in summer, when the yellow, golden sun would rise up from the shoulder of the mountain. Mountain and open sea would be the colour of gold with the brightness of the weather. The fish would be coming in on the quay and shoaling outside in the mouth of the strand and in Yellow Island Shore. You wouldn't see ever at a race or a fair any sight to beat it, when there would be

A currach off the Great Blasket

above twenty currachs in the drive round it.

That life is gone and we're hoping every day to be taken out of this place. But I suppose it is a case of the spit ready for the venison and the deer not killed yet, because the people we're depending on to take us out have enough to do themselves. Maybe, with God's help, this life could change yet and the Island would rise again. There are people here who think they have a great life of it in other places. That isn't true. The peace of God is here always. There is neither trouble nor strife here.

If a man climbed up the shoulder of the mountain on a fine summer's evening, the fragrance and sweetness of the air would scatter the memory of any sorrow or torment plaguing him and he would go back home in the bloom of health again. It is often I would take my rest on the shoulder of the highest mountain, looking at the beauty of the heights around me and listening to the murmur of the waves. It is often, too, that the same loveliness would cause me to stretch back with my belly up to the sun.

But, my sharp sorrow, the thief came – age, the smooth trickster, and he stole on me unawares. I see today, as I imagine them, the people that were there in my youth. My father is alive again before me, talking to Seán Fada. I see Seán Eibhlís and the Yank and Eoghan Mór conversing together in the same old way. I see the old ruined house where Seán Eibhlís used to live and where I spent my young days. Look how my thoughts run back across the long years that have passed over me. The little ruined house is there all by itself still. It is well I remember seeing a drove of grand boys and girls coming and going to that house. But they all passed away, without the least thought that that's the way things would be. My blessing and the blessing of God on them, until we meet together again in the eternal kingdom of heaven.

CHAPTER 24

A Change in my Life again

I HAVE a different life now. I have a big, wide house and my own work to do. Without any doubt the days of my youth are gone. I get a cross word from no one and I'm at no one's beck and call. It isn't the same class of life I have now that I had when I was across the sea in a foreign land, where I was held in a cat's grip by a foreman who was more ignorant than myself. Now there is nothing to bother me. I haven't a worry in the wide world. My mother is hardy and strong and she looks after the house. My brothers and sisters are in America, all that are left of them.

I got an assurance from my brother Muiris that I could make free with the house and land, that he would never come back himself to interfere with me. I would never stop him coming, of course, whenever he wished. But he didn't want to put me off any plan I might think of to better or improve myself. That is, if I wanted to marry, he wouldn't stand in my way.

But that was the one thing I had no means of doing here. No doubt there were plenty of girls good enough for me and the fault wasn't on them that I didn't marry, but on myself. To my way of thinking, if I married on the Island I'd only be a drudge all my days. I have to admit that I was fond of a girl once, but it wasn't meant for us to go under the yoke of marriage. We were young then and it is easy to bewilder the young. She didn't like to marry on the Island for she thought it was a poor place in which to spend her life.

It is often since then I think she was entirely right. For, as the years were going past, it was becoming firmly fixed in my mind that we would be better off not to marry. But by the same token it is easy to upset a person, for when that much went against me, it was how I decided to go to America to see if I could forget her at all. But, my sorrow, it was going hard on me ever and always, until that girl married a couple of years ago. I'm glad she has what she wanted. The same woman will never be as well off as I would wish her to be, whatever life is in store for myself.

I remember, when we were both young, that I used to take her out walking with me in front of her father and mother. We would walk and walk until we reached the top of the hill. The height wouldn't bother us. We were like a little brother and sister together. I would pick every bright flower growing on the mountain and tie them in a button-hole in front of her dress to please her. We were young and everything looked good to us. The hardship of this life wasn't troubling us at all. We didn't like to be under any control, only to be free without a fetter always.

I'd sooner see her shining forehead coming against me on the road, than to see the sun rising on a lovely morning in Autumn. But she was a stranger in the place, and when she went home she never came back to the Island again. As I said before, she is married since and is doing well. She has a nice piece of land and a good husband and I don't begrudge her that.

I never married, but I'm not the only one on the Island. It looks as if there will be a crowd of us in the same state before long. Marriage went astray with many more besides me. But there is only the one cure for regret and that is to kill it with patience.

CHAPTER 25

How Life went to the bad on the Island

IT seems that life will never again be as good as it was for, as the years go past, I'm getting it into my head that there's a hard life in front of me. I was pulling away fine through life until now. I had neither family nor care and, as I said before, I had the house and place all to myself. There was no one to interfere with me and nothing to stop me doing whatever I wanted.

Before my father died, God's own blessing on his soul, he gave me every guidance in such a way that he turned me into a clever handyman about the house. He taught me how to farm and how to knit nets and every other thing that concerns a man of the house.

I have courage and joy in my heart yet, and my mind is as strong as it ever was. But when my thoughts go back through the grand happy years, lost and gone for ever, my spirit droops and that is no wonder for I saw a comfortable life:

> From the day of our father's funeral
> We have seen neither peace nor pleasure.
> With every sword-stroke smiting us
> We were scattered to the world.
>
> One man of us went East,
> To the West the next hurried.
> On our fort and our good village
> We all turned our backs.
>
> So, we spent many years,
> Homeless, without fort or settlement,

Until we were destroyed by death
And the game went astray.

We showed we lacked sense,
To turn back on our country.
Many a man and gentle graceful girl
Has comfort there today.

All the wealth of this life,
Its gold and its chattels,
All of it would not satisfy us,
Great though its amount.

No household in the great world,
From the Red Sea to Inis Fáil,
Was better than we were then,
Until we lost chieftain and retinue.

A great desire seized us,
We abandoned our wealth and share.
Fate turned against us,
It left me here deserted.

Here I am today, reader, going back along the lonesome
boreen of my thoughts. I see Barra Lia west from me, where
all the fish used to be killed in my young days. The sky is as
blue above it as ever it was. I can see the brown heather on
top of the heights and there are golden castles on the horizon.
The little quay is at the foot of the cliff yet, where the misfortunes used to be in the evening, putting their nets into the
little boats to go to Barra Lia fishing. The poor misfortunes
are not there today and the only signs of them left are the
marks of their hobnailed boots on the grey stones of the quay.

It is many a fine evening my father was there, God rest his
soul, and it is myself that used to be delighted when he would

take me out in the currach. The first day ever I went into it, when I felt it swaying, I thought it was in a big cradle I was. When I said this to my father he started laughing.

'On my soul,' said Seán Fada, who was sitting on the thwart next to my father, ''tis you that put the proper name on her. It is a long time since anyone baptized her so well!'

I would lift my head to look around and see Páidín Mhuiris in another currach beside me, holding two oars and he pulling away. But my father wouldn't let me have the oars at all, for fear I might drop the thole-pins in the sea. I would be in a sulk, and no wonder, when I saw Páidín and the sport he was having with the oars.

There used to be great ree-rah and commotion altogether there, but the men passed away one after another, may God grant eternal rest to their souls in heaven.

I remember well how myself and my brother Pádraig used to go to the hill hunting and bring a fine bundle of rabbits back home with us in the evening. My brother Muiris never went with us. He was a good hunter on the sea, surely, and it is often he would be out early and late.

We had a grand gay life of it, though we had no high notions. We had neither wealth nor riches, but all the same we weren't short of a thing in the world. God helped us, praise be to Him for ever.

It was often Nell Mhór used to drop in to us, with her small wooden bowl under her apron, to borrow flour from my mother. Whenever she was caught in a fix, my mother gave it to her and that carried her on until God's help came. We spent our lives in the shadow of one another. When my father was short of anything, he used to send me back to Micil looking for it.

I remember well how myself and the small gorsoons going to school with me often had a fight. We would be playing and having sport together afterwards. It wasn't anything we held against each other, but we had the youth and the high spirits.

I can't see a single one of those boys today. It is far and wide we're scattered. Some are married here and more are married there. Some have died. It is the same with the big-hearted, pleasant girls that were there. Those that are still living have their own care.

But I'm like Oisín[1] after the Fianna now, gazing out through the window and thinking sadly about all these things. What runs in my head sitting here is that the day is over for people on the Island, unless there is a change in the world soon.

[1] Poet-son of Fionn Mac Cumhail, leader of legendary warrior-band, the Fianna

CHAPTER 26

How the Islanders were clearing off and settling down on the Mainland

IT was little I thought when I came home from America that the people would leave the Island and go to live on the mainland. There was a rumour going round that some of them were leaving, but you wouldn't believe a word of it. It was the strange news surely, for where would the poor people go when they left the place they had? That was the question. But when they gathered themselves off and got the place they had marked out for themselves, then there was all the talk.

'Wisha, Peig, my heart,' said Bríde Lia to my mother one evening, when I was after coming from the hill, 'isn't life hard, to say that we have to leave our cabin in the end, fond and all of it as we are.'

'You poor woman,' said my mother, 'I suppose that's what's in store for you.'

'True for you, Peig. Nothing on earth would get it out of my head that all these things are laid down for us, from the day we came into the world till the day we leave it. I had no notion at all sure, woman, that Paddy would ever consent to leave this place, until the last nail would be driven into his coffin.'

'Whisht, will you, woman,' said my mother, 'wasn't it the last thought in my head that Paddy would do the likes. Beyond all the men in the world I believed he had some splink of sense, but I'm afraid he hasn't. It is ye that had the nice, sheltered, comfortable house here, far from the wind of the sea and, on top of it all, ye never knew hunger.'

'To be sure, my dear, it isn't hunger or thirst that is driving us out. But when we see people leaving, we want to do the same thing. Would you have any wish to leave this place, Peig?'

'Wisha, I suppose I would if I got any place that suited me, but I don't see any notion of it in the son. I think he prefers to stay where he is for a while yet anyway.'

'He's right, Peig. There's time enough for him to leave. If I had my way, I'd stand my ground another while too. But it's Paddy that wears the trousers, not myself. I swear by anything you like, woman of my heart, that I won't live a month in the place where we're going. Paddy tells me that I won't have any sight of the sea and that the strand will be too far away from me. Yerra, Peig, I have no way of living there. I'm too used to dilisk[1] and bairneachs,[2] and would you believe what I'm going to tell you, I never heard sweeter music than the thunder of the waves breaking on the strand.'

'Have sense for yourself, Bríde, ye'll have a different story when ye go to live in the new house.'

'May God grant that, Peig. The fear is on me because a strange place is always treacherous.'

'Listen, woman, "God is stronger than hope." Aren't we all depending on God's mercy every single day. Take note, woman, that it is according to His true holy will all this world goes round. There isn't a thing small or great hidden anywhere that He doesn't know, even the secret thoughts of our own hearts. It is amazement and wonder to you to be leaving this pace. Don't wonder at it at all. I'm telling you it was in store for you, and if it is the cause of your death itself, you must welcome it.'

'I suppose so, wisha. It isn't any fear of death I have, Peig, but it is how I'm lonesome to be leaving the place. I had great ease here and I had good neighbours too. I've spent over forty years amongst them and I never yet saw two of them fighting. That's not the case with other villages. From

---

[1] Edible sea-plant.   [2] Limpets, barnacles.

what I hear they have the stone in the sleeve for one another always.

'But it isn't that that's bothering me, but when I think of my own small house, where I used to be eating and drinking. What's laying bare the lonesome thoughts altogether in my heart is that the day will come soon when the birds of the wild will be nesting there. That little house, Peig, where there was the gay company always, the blessing of God on the souls of the dead! It was many the day that Seán Fada himself spent there with us and he was a great man for the crack. Didn't I see himself and Pats Mór on the point of striking one another over Nan Mhór, and the pair of them bucking widowers. Nan was a fine strong, brave girl at that time. There wasn't her like in the Island or the next parish. The two of them were out of their heads altogether over her, but she didn't marry either of them nor did she marry at all. She spent all her life as an old maid.'

'I'd say, Bríde, that it was easy for Nan to get a man.'

'Yerra, God love you, it was easy. Nan would get a man for every one of her fingers. At that time it was how they were eyeing one another to see which of them would have the luck to get her. But everyone has his own faults, God help us. She hadn't the smallest thought of marrying till she fell in the tight grip of the years. I heard her saying then that there was a curse on anyone who wouldn't marry when they got the chance of it.'

'I declare to you, Bríde, that she was right in that much. A woman on her own is a great pity, especially when the age is coming on her.'

'Oh, there's no contrariness in the world like it, Peig. There's something or other always bothering them and the likes of them are very hard to please, too.'

'They can't help it, Bríde.'

'They can't I suppose, Peig. "The man on the ditch is the best hurler." It would be very easy for her to find others like her. I had a young sister and the same thing happened to her. She was one of the lovely women of Ventry parish. Five offers of marriage came to her one Shrovetide and what do you say to her, woman, but didn't she refuse each and every one of them.

'My poor father, may God have mercy on him, was tormented from her, because she had no wish for any of them. For, on my soul, every one of those five boys was good enough for her. They all had full and plenty and the lucky girl that married one of them wouldn't know hunger. But at that time, my sister's nose would run blood if any one of them was mentioned to her. There was this fault or that fault on them but, believe me, Peig, it was on herself all the fault was in the end, for those boys married and the days went by until my sister became bent and useless. She was full of pity for herself then, when she could see other women and the comfortable life they had of it.'

'Oh, my dear, it is true that we only learn when it is too late. But I suppose it never entered the poor girl's head that she wouldn't get some man.'

'I don't know, wisha, Peig, we would have preferred it if she had listened to my father and married, for the poor man was tormented entirely when she went against him. For that reason, when Paddy came south to Ventry parish to ask for me to be his wife, I didn't want to refuse him for fear my father wouldn't like it. I found no fault with Paddy, but I had no wish to come and live on the Island. To my way of thinking it was very hemmed in and the sea used to frighten me, but soon afterwards I got a great liking for the place.'

'Wisha, my life on you, Bride, you did well not to refuse your father.'

'I had no complaint against him ever, Peig, the place suited me fine. But it looks as if I'll have to leave it again.'

'May luck go with you, Bride, and may God give you a long life in comfort in the new house.'

'Amen, and the same to you, Peig, and I hope to see yourself out on the mainland.'

'Maybe, with God's help, Bríde. The likes of us have no business here any more.'

And the pair of them strolled out side by side.

CHAPTER 27

The big Aeroplanes and the Fright they gave the Women of the Island the first time they saw them

ONE evening Máire Chaol landed in the door to us. Máire was a next door neighbour of ours, and a good woman too. On my word, it would have been easier for me to understand a Greek than her, she had such a rush of talk.

'Steady, Máire,' said I, 'what put the fright on you? One would think 'twas how you saw a ghost.'

'Yerra, God of Miracles, man, wasn't it a dreadful time of it. I was for ages listening to accounts of the great aeroplanes that were made in England and Germany, but I never saw them rightly until today. I didn't think I'd live an hour when I heard the noise coming on me through the sky. I looked up, but where was the thing making the noise? I didn't see a whack, because of all the mist. Then I tried to run, but before I reached the house the great black monster was on my heels. Great God, what a fright! I'll never be in the better of it.

'I thought the red fire would be pitched down on top of us any minute. Isn't the city they make for to be pitied? They don't leave a bit of it standing with their bombs. Aren't the poor women and children to be pitied when that mob are above them in the sky, tossing down their shells of fire on top of them without rhyme or reason?'

'They're to be pitied, surely, Máire. The same aeroplanes have caused havoc already. It's many the person that's help-less after them that was having the fine life of it,' said I.

'I'm afraid this war will put an end to the world entirely, Micheál.'

'Hush your mouth, woman, have sense for yourself. "God

is stronger than hope," as Peig says. We'll be hearing a different story before long. There's small danger but they'll make
some agreement when they've run out of war material.'

'Maybe so, with God's help, Micheál. There's nothing better than a settlement. What brought me here now was to get
a loan of the small can full of meal from your mother. I'm out
of my wits with the hens; they wouldn't plant their beaks on
the bare potatoes.'

'Wisha, Máire, you couldn't do a better thing with them
than to put them in the skillet for yourself. There won't be a
grain of meal to be had for gold or silver and the flour itself
won't be too plentiful, from what I hear.'

'God save us for ever, what will we do at all?'

'Oh! that's it for you, Máire, live as long as you can now.'

My mother rose and filled the can with meal for her.

'Here,' said she, 'and there aren't three cans full at the
bottom of the bag after you, but let us put the evil day on the
long finger.'

'God go with you, Peig, it is from you that comes best,' and
she bustled off out and on my word there wasn't a soldier in
King George's army who was more afraid of the war in his
heart than herself.

CHAPTER 28

Páidín Mhuiris comes home from England

ONE fine morning when I got up, the weather was beautiful
and the sun shining brightly on every single thing. I told my
mother I'd go to Dunquin to bring back a little supply for the
week.

'You might as well, son,' she said. 'You won't always have
the day fine.'

I picked up my thole-pins.

'Don't forget to buy a pair of black laces for me to put in
my boots.'

'I won't, if I remember them.'

'Make sure of it, boy,' she said.

When I went to the slip, Muiris Keane and Tomás O'Donlevy were going out. They had the currach afloat before me.

The channel between the Island and Dunquin is good and
long when the weather is bad. But it is very pleasant when
the calm is there. It is like a bay.

It is a dead heart that the balmy air of the sea wouldn't lift
the gloom from it on a fine day. I was looking away south
from me towards Iveragh. Soon I saw hundreds and
thousands of sea-birds coming towards me from the South,
flying this side and that, hunting for small fishes. Muiris and
the other man were chatting away.

'By my palms, Tomás,' said Muiris, 'the fish are shoaling
in the Sound today.'

'They are, boy. It looks promising, whatever.'

'I don't remember that I saw such a sight of sea-birds ever
before,' said Muiris.

'It would be hard for you to see a sight that would beat
what you have in front of you now,' said Tomás. 'Look,

they're all on top of each other. The whole sea is full of them south to Creek Mouth and from that west to Bray Head and what's more extraordinary, each bird has his own music going.'

'He has,' said Muiris. 'Each one has his own nature laid out for him.'

'It seems so,' said Tomás.

'Yes, man,' said Muiris, 'there's nothing more powerful than nature.'

The pair of them went on chatting about the birds and their nature until we put in at Great Cliff. Who should be above on the quay before us but Páidín Mhuiris? He was after coming home from England. I ran to him and knocked a hundred shakes out of his hand. My heart seemed to burst with joy when I saw my old butty again.

When I had eaten my supper that evening, I strolled east to call on Páidín. The house was full of people, small and big. It was a custom of the Island people to go and welcome the stranger. Of course Páidín was a stranger that night. There wasn't a thing he put his eye on that he didn't make a wonder of it. Even the very floor itself in the house seemed odd to him. He nearly fell over on top of his head with the bulging eyes in him. It wasn't the same as the fine houses he was used to during the four years he had spent in London. We had a laugh and a scoff at him, believe me. But it was all equal to him. He was as satisfied as if he were in a big drawing-room in London.

'It is true, Dad,' he said, 'that there's no place like home.'

'True, son,' said Muiris, 'the place where a person is born is the place where he prefers to be.'

'Though this is the most remote village in Ireland,' said Páidín, 'it is where I prefer to be this night, for there's no uproar or noise or commotion here, only peace and God's grace. There's no burning or scorching here, like there is in England.'

Dunquin Parish

'The poor people in England are greatly to be pitied in the world that's in it now,' said Muiris.

'They are greatly to be pitied, surely, Dad,' said he. 'You'd see the crowds out on the streets every day since the war started, with no place to go for the night, and their houses burnt to the ground by the big aeroplanes. They come over in black droves above them in the sky and toss down their balls of fire. The burning they cause is a terror to the world. The poor people are frightened out of their lives by them. Often they're chased away, but they come back again and again.'

'Not coming before you in your story, Páidín, did you hear any word over amongst them at all that the people of England were going to make a settlement?' asked Seán Carney.

'I didn't, Seán. 'Tis how they're preparing themselves for the big battle that's to come. They're expecting the enemy to land any day. It looks as if they would rather fall in battle than let the enemy win. But there are plenty in England who would prefer peace. There's great havoc done there already. There isn't a city in the length and breadth of England today that hasn't the marks of the fire well on it. They say that there will be scarcity there if the war lasts long more.'

'There's a danger there will, and many places else besides,' said Muiris, rising. 'The night's gone, men,' said he.

'I suppose it is,' said Seán Carney, 'but we must only add a piece of the morning to it.'

CHAPTER 29

My Mother's good Advice to me

THE time was slipping by me slowly and stubbornly. I'd be contented for one while and not contented for another. It was often I told my mother that there was a hard life in store for us. But the answer she would make was: 'Have patience for yourself, my son, and whatever is in store for you, you'll receive. You think, boy, that people with worldly wealth have life to their own liking. Don't feel any envy for them, son. Those people are not free from the troubles of the world. When I was a toddler growing up, all I had to eat was scraps. That was the time when the poor were needy and hungry. 'Tis well I remember how I gave many a day working for other people and all I had for it was a small bite of food. I'd have to be working hard from morning to night for that same, the way 'tis no wonder, d'you see, son, for your mother to be showing her years.'

'I suppose, wisha, there was no pity for a servant girl in those days.'

'Wisha, my torment, the last mistress where I was in service had neither pity nor understanding for me, anyhow. If I told you any different, I'd be putting a thumper of a lie on her. Would you believe, son, that my blood shivers when I think of the hardship I went through. It is seldom I made a boast about the length of time I spent there. I'm telling you there was no regret on me the day that I left it. I never saw a bad day since, great thanks to God.

'My life is nearly done now and soon I'll be having the long sleep without waking, despite the best I can do. My advice to you, son, is to mind your Faith well. Avoid evil always and God will help you. Don't be dissatisfied if this

thing or that crosses you. Understand, son, that you can't
spend your life the way you want it yourself. Many things
will cross you in the run of your life and you will have to have
patience. Without the patience, you have no way of coming
through the trials of this life. It is God Himself, praise be to
Him for ever, who gives us the patience to endure all these
things that are laid down for us by Him in the stretch of our
life.'

'For that reason don't have envy of anyone, for there's no
one without his own small crosses. Your mother, I promise
you, is a woman who got but little solace in the run of this
life. I've dragged my way through it, suffering affliction and
sorrow, but the Sacred High King gave help to me. The thing
that always troubled me the most, son, was what I'm going
to say to you. It is often I prayed with all my heart to the
King of Glory that neither myself nor yeerselves would do
anything out of the way on Him, that would separate us from
one another on the great day of judgment, but that we would
all be in the one company in God's Kingdom, the way we
were in this life. Only God has the help to give and maybe
I would be granted my prayer. It would be well-deserved, after
spending our while in this vale of tears, to be all in the one
company in heaven. God, praise be to Him for ever, will
never bestow on us a jewel that I'd prefer above it. He won't
fail us, son.

'I have love for God ever since I was a little child. Everything He created was a solace to me, even sorrow itself. 'Tis
said by our blessed clergy to us that every tear that's shed in
pity for Christ's passion is a pearl.

'For this reason, all that's in the things of this world is only
emptiness. It is folly for us not to store our treasure away
where the moths won't eat it and rust will not come on it
ever.

'Be a man always wherever you go. Help the weak if you
can and don't let the sun go down on your anger.

'You're here today. You might be far away from here tomorrow. There were men as strong and brave as you here, but where are they today, God help us! They were laid out in the same way that you will be, and I will be.

'This world is coming very hard on us lately, but don't mind it, the sky will clear yet and the sun will shine bright again. The sooner life takes a turn upwards the better. All I hear from morning to night is war, war, war, this body advancing and the other body retreating. There's danger on sea and land. There's terror and dread on everyone. Don't mind it, son; the higher the gale, the nearer the help. The Sacred High King will bring us safe, sound and secure through it. Don't have any fear. There's no danger to us from it with God's help. When we will be least expecting it, that's when God's peace will come down on earth again.

'Pride and haughtiness were the cause of all this work. Haven't you heard that a whole shipful are drowned because of one person? The people who are doing all this evil will be swept out of the world in time. I promise you they will, and the only traces left of them will be the mark of the bad deed they did. Maybe a headstone will be put over some of them. One man here and another man there will say that they were the great soldiers. But, my torment, there will be more men in their place who won't be remembered at all, whose glory is short-lived. I promise you that it will be told in the histories of the world about the character and deeds of those other men, about the great victories they won over the enemy and the destruction they caused. But what will they gain by it if they have the bush in the gap[1] in front of them by and by? It would have been for their good to have put a rein on their pride and have given the back of their hand to the sin that was urging them on to do evil while they were alive.'

'That's true,' said I, 'but isn't it hard to put fright or fear

---

[1] Their entrance to heaven barred.

on a hardy, strong, brave man, when all that comes between him and his night's sleep is to defend his country from his enemy.'

'Whisper, son, we wouldn't be any the better for it if we talked about it for ever for a story.

'Would you mind at all going on the strand to bring me back a little bag of sand to sprinkle on the floor. The ass is back in the field. You'd be better off doing something than to be sprawled there yarning.'

'You're right,' said I, and I took the little bag with me and went pacing along the road west.

CHAPTER 30

The Death of Seán Dhiarmaid – The Wake and the Trouble that followed putting him into God's Ground

SEÁN DHIARMAID died today, may they be safe and well where 'tis told. The man of the big heart we called him. We were all fond of poor Seán, for he never let anyone away from the door without easing his trouble. He would give a helping hand in any way he could at all. He had a nice, dry, comfortable house beside the Boreen of the Dead. Any man going the road, Seán would call him into the house. There wasn't his match to be found in his day. Signs on it, we were all very sorry after him.

I swallowed down the cup of tea in a hurry to go to the wake-house. When I arrived it was how the corpse was laid out on the bed. There was a big table placed at the foot and candles lighting on it. A man from the village was sitting on a chair at the head of the table and he cutting tobacco and putting it on a plate beside him. Stretched the length of the house were two planks and props under them at the two ends, so as the man coming in could sit down at his ease.

The two benches were nearly full when I landed. There was only a gap here and there. The man coming in would make straight for the gap ever and always, until every space was full. The women were around the fire, chatting away pleasantly together. Much of the night hadn't gone when a curlew let out a cry.

'The blessing of God on the souls of the dead that have left us, what's that?' said an old woman bestirring herself near the fire.

'That was one of the mountain curlews, woman,' said Tomás Mór Carney. 'Tomorrow will be fine, with God's help. Announcing good weather to us is what that bird is doing.'

The curlew gave another cry.

'There's something wrong with the bird,' she said again. 'If he weren't astray in some way, he wouldn't be crying out like that at this hour of the night.'

'The loveliness of the night that's affecting him, woman,' said Eoghan O'Sullivan. 'Don't think anything of it. It isn't announcing any harm to us he is. That bird is always crying like that on a fine night.'

The curlew let out another cry.

'Oh! the Cross of God between us and harm,' said she, rising to her feet. 'That bird is announcing something. Where is the bottle of holy water, Máire?'

I have it here,' said Máire, handing her the bottle. 'Shake a little drop on me, Bríde, for the souls of the dead, since 'tis in your hands.'

'If we had a little sup of tea swallowed, women,' said Siobhán, 'we'd be better able to change the story. You'd better rise, Nell, and wet it for us. The men will drink a little sup of it too. They're in need of it, since we haven't any other little warm drop.'

'Faith, wisha, I won't refuse you, Siobhán,' said Nell, rising. 'We all have a great mind for it the same as yourself. The men needn't go by us if they like. The man that's laid out tonight wouldn't mind in the least drinking a pot of tea at a time like this. No, faith, but twenty of them. He was a tidy housekeeper, Siobhán, that God may make the road easy for his soul this night. On my oath he was, wisha, and a man of the big heart too, and a man who didn't cause a neighbour's child to cry ever. I don't suppose the same man ever spoke a cross word out of his mouth to anyone, whatever cause he might have for it.'

'He didn't, wisha, Nell. A quiet, gentle man poor Seán

was, God rest his soul tonight. Oh, isn't death the thief! Isn't it he that steals on top of us unexpected. We never thought he'd die so soon.'

'Oh, my dear woman, Siobhán, that thief steals on top of us often unexpected. 'Tis as well for us to lay the table. You bring the cups, Bríde. Leave the rest to myself and Siobhán.'

'Here, little girls, take yeer fill of the jam,' said Nell.

'There's an edge on our teeth for it,' said Cáitín Thomáis Mhóir. 'On my oath, 'tis long since we saw the likes.'

'Hurry on with ye now, children dear. Siobhán will be starting to say the rosary for Seán Dhiarmaid's soul and all the souls of the dead.'

We all knelt down and Siobhán started. But before the rosary was finished the little red cockerel hopped out of the hen-coop and crew. If I were to be hanged for it, I couldn't help myself laughing at Nell, when I saw her making the sign of the Cross over herself and darting at the cockerel with the bowl of a clay pipe she held in her fist.

'Wisha, that you may lie there till you're weak from it, what a time for you to be crowing!'

She caught a grip of the cockerel by the windpipe and flung him into the coop amongst the hens.

'Stay there now, you rascal, and if you hop out again, I'll put you in a place where you will stay!'

It was bright day when I came home, for whatever bravery was in me, I didn't care to face home on my own. It was laid down that it wasn't right for anyone to leave a wake-house without another person by his side and so I stayed where I was till morning. The day was grand and fine and the people in the wake-house were fixing themselves up to go to the funeral. South to Ventry church-yard Seán Dhiarmaid was taken on the shoulders of the men, for it was there his people for seven generations had been put under the clay. They didn't bother with any vehicle to carry the coffin across the hill, for the help was there.

We buried him in the holy graveyard amongst his friends and relations. He'll stay there sleeping quietly in everlasting peace, until the Angel blows the trumpet on God's judgment day. Hunger and thirst are no danger to him from now on, or cold from the North or heat from the South. All his kind deeds are under the headstone with him, that they may do good to his soul. All he possessed was left to Siobhán and on my oath it wasn't a bad woman that had it, for she took the hunger away from many a person. It was often said that God would grant her heart's fill to her and He did, for Seán Dhiarmaid was neither thriftless nor poor. He had money in the bank and he left it all to Siobhán and, faith, it was her due. She had the best right to it and no one else. It was she that looked after him until he died. It doesn't matter to her what corner she settles herself in from now on. She won't have a shortage in the world. It is many a woman of the village that is envious of Siobhán today and no wonder, for this is the life where everyone is fond of the money.

As soon as the last shovelful of earth was clamped on Seán Dhiarmaid's grave, everyone was heading for home as fast as he could. Believe me too, that it wasn't any piece of bread earned easy we had until we reached home. The day was grand and fine and nearly everyone in the village went to the funeral. But it wasn't long before it turned squally and a swell rose in the sea. The currachs could make no headway. The tide and wind were against them. We didn't know what was the best thing to do. Some of the men said that it would be better to turn off for Beg-inish, that the wind and tide wouldn't be too much against them there and, if they couldn't push on, then they'd stay there till morning. That was agreed and we turned for Beg-inish. But, God of Miracles! that was the time there was the fright. However hard we tried, the sea was pouring into the currach despite us. The women with us were shaking with fear. They were in dread of their lives, and no mistake, to judge by their olagóning. But Micil spoke:

'Put away yeer olagóning. Aren't all our lives in danger the same as ye? Pull away with you, Tadhg; take no notice of them for women. Any boat that has women in it is sunk, but the blame wasn't on them but on ourselves, that we didn't leave them behind on the quay. We're making good headway men, thanks be to God. The worst place for it was south at Scologue Sound. If we'd gone on south two lengths more of the currach we wouldn't have south or north now, but the job is done, along with God's help.'

'It is, Micil,' said Tadhg. 'I suppose it was God, praise be to Him for ever, that put it into our heads to turn so quickly. The other eight currachs turned too when they saw us.'

'It was well they did, Tadhg. God was thankful to them; if they hadn't done so they'd be drowned by this time.'

Soon the olagóning stopped. When we reached Beg-inish everyone was shaking himself up again. We were drenched, but we weren't bothered over that, so long as we were free from danger. Speech was coming back to the women too. Micil reddened his pipe and gave Tadhg a pull of it.

There wasn't a man, woman or child in the village who didn't go to the funeral, but was waiting for us at the quay when we arrived back. They were terrified when they saw the currachs in Scologue Sound, that dreadful day, thinking we were all drowned. That's what we thought ourselves too, and no wonder. But God arranges everything for the best, praise be to Him for ever. That wasn't the place marked out for our death, for it was near a miracle how hard the men strained, crossing the Sound that day. Believe me, reader, we'll be re-membering Seán Dhiarmaid's funeral a while yet, for it was a day beyond days, when everyone who was there had given himself up for lost.

CHAPTER 31

How a Person's Life passes away

A PERSON'S life races on in the exact same way that a wind
lifts the mist from the shoulder of a mountain. My life too is
nearly done. The gladness and gaiety, the run and the jump,
the laughter and brightness and mirth are gone from me. My
sharp grief, they will pay me a visit no more. It is a big gap
in my life that these lovely pearls are lost, for a spool would
not wind faster than the way the last days of our life slip
away from us. Death with the grace of our Holy Creator will
put a sleep without waking on us. Other people will get pleasure from our share and we shall not be there to frown on
them. We are greatly mistaken that we do not make use of
the loan of this life for the short time we are there, despite the
best we can do. If we put a stop to the foolish deeds of our
lives and went by the teaching the Holy Clergy gave us, there
is little danger that we would not possess the eternal Kingdom that is promised us after this. Is it not to be seen clearly
by me that nothing lasts in this world except the grace of
God? Is it not often in the course of my life that God had
mercy on me? I would go within a finger's throw of death,
when He would lay His glorious eye down on me. He would
put the danger past me.

O God of Grace, Whose goodness is without end, grant us
to love You in this life, so as nothing would be coming between ourselves and You that would make You have disgust
and hatred for us. For all this life will come to nothing and all
that will be there will be You, O God of truth and right, in
Whom we put all our trust and hope. Be merciful to us, O
Lord God, and guide our path in this vale of tears. Do not let
that foul enemy who travels through this life lead us astray.

Is there not many a person on the wrong road yet, who never
got knowledge or guidance about Your great glory or Your
sacred gifts? They are lying in the darkness. Glory to You, O
Holy Father, Who lit the glorious light in our midst. For love
of us You sent Your Own Son to rescue and save us. Should
we not be glad that Jesus came for love of us down from
heaven? Is it not we that are tormented, when small things
cross us and we knowing well that every trouble we accept
with patience for God's sake is a pearl in our eternal crown?
Christ died for all of us on top of the Hill of Calvary to win
eternal happiness for us after this in heaven. Praise and
thanks to You, O Lord God, when the need is greatest, that
is when you are nearest to us.

The spiritual joy that comes like sunshine on my troubled
mind is like honey to my tormented heart. In a short while, it
is as joyful as it ever was. A good confession is a wonderful
thing. Am I not clean again in the sight of God? My heart is
free from the black troubles of this life. Before now hell was
blazing up in front of me. Nothing would give me peace of
mind. Is it not well I know Your Holy help, O Lord, for it
was often I was held in the grip of black clouds of sorrow and
no way out for me except Your help. I have this much to say,
that God helps the weak and grants us peace of mind. I remember well when I was a lad hearing my father and
Diarmaid Thomáis saying that there would be a big change
before the end of the world came. It seems they were right,
for there is no good in life for a long time because of wars,
and it seems that many will lose their lives before there is an
end to them, but God's will be done.

CHAPTER 32

Thinking to myself

THE thing I'm thinking about now is a day long ago, when our mother sent us to fetch two panniers of turf. It was a great year. There was a glow and shine on everything that God created. My father himself was fine and strong and all of us were happy together. My mother settled that Pádraig and myself should go back to Mountain's Loop to fetch two panniers of turf. We had no ass that summer, for our big white ass had fallen over a cliff. We were not inclined to go, for all the lads of the village were down below on the strand playing football and we preferred beyond anything at that time to be there amongst them. But faith, we had no business going against our mother.

When we were ready we made for the road. But, as the old saying has it, 'going to the king's palace is not the same as coming from it.' That was the same case with myself and my brother Pádraig. We were hardy and tough in those days, and it would take us no time at all to walk to Mountain's Loop, or to a place further away. It didn't take us half an hour to go there. When we shaped up properly to the work, we filled the two panniers with grand dry turf, but whatever put it into my brother's head to go hunting, he wouldn't rest until I went with him . Off with us back across Narrow Glen and down Shoulder of Heather. It wasn't walking we were but trotting, till we reached the foot of Two Glens. The black dog we had poked his head into a big hole and straightened his tail.

'There's a rabbit in the hole,' said Pádraig.

We started rooting and tearing up the ground. We lifted two rabbits out of the hole. That gave us fresh courage to tackle another hole. We were rooting and tearing away until the stars were to be seen in the sky. We had twelve fine rabbits dangling on a cord coming home. But when we came to Mountain's Loop the two panniers weren't there before us. That was the time for the hubbub with the two of us; how would we give satisfaction to our mother when we got home? We asked God to put us on the right road and help us. To tell the truth, we had no wish to go home without bringing the turf with us. In the heel of the hunt, we decided to settle ourselves down in the rick of turf until morning. We thought that maybe it was thieves that stole the turf and that they would come back for two more panniers full. Whatever Pádraig made his mind up to do, there was no use going against him. We made a hole in the mouth of the rick and the two of us hid inside it. On my soul, reader, when I think of the strain I went through that night, between the lonesomeness and dread that were on me, my blood shivers. It seems that hardship and distress follow the man who hasn't his wits about him always. The night was passing and no one was coming to steal the turf. But by the same token, no one was short of it that summer. They all had plenty of firing. In the end we heard people talking. I recognized my father's voice amongst them.

'God save us,' he said, 'they're finished now or never. There's no one who would be alive on Island Hill this time of the night, who wouldn't be making for home. But, my sorrow, they are not able to come.

'On my soul, they are,' Diarmaid said. "Tis how they were hunting until the darkness fell on them.'

'If that were the story, Diarmaid, they would be here to meet us once night fell.'

'I suppose so, but the pair of them didn't fall down a cliff together, and another thing, Patsy, the dog himself would have come home. But they're alive yet in some place and the dog is there along with them.'

'You're right, Diarmaid, they're alive yet,' said Seán Fada. 'If they were dead, as Patsy says, the dog would come home.'

'We're alive and kicking yet!' said Pádraig, jumping out of the rick.

'Look where they are, Diarmaid,' said my father.

'Didn't I tell you, Patsy, that they were alive in some place,' said Diarmaid.

'You did, man, but 'twas hard for me to give in to you. Wisha, a pair of boots on you, Pádraig!' my father said. That was the kind of a curse he used to have always. 'What kept ye here so long?'

'Our two panniers that were stolen from us, Dad,' said he, 'and the pair of us stayed here minding the rick until the thief would come again. But ye're the thieves that came interfering with us.'

'I pity you greatly, son. It wasn't any thief that stole the turf. It was myself and Muiris that brought it home. We strolled this way shortly after ye went on the hill and when we saw the two panniers full I said to Muiris that we'd better bring them home for ye'd be worn out from hunting.'

'You were right, too, Dad. We were played out.'

'The story is fine now, but yeer poor mother will be terrified.'

'There's great danger to her,' said Diarmaid, 'so long as they're alive,' and he reddened his pipe beside the rick. We came home then. My father brought the bundle of rabbits with him.

'Faith, Patsy,' said Seán Fada, pulling his coat up around his ears, 'there's no limit to young people.'

'There isn't, my dear man,' said my father. 'It was little thought I had when I left the house that it would be inside a rick in Mountain's Loop I'd find this pair.'

'I suppose you thought you were finished with them, you poor man,' said Seán.

'I thought, Seán, that they were as dead as my father that

The Poet tells a folk-tale to a summer school in West Kerry

was in Ballynahoun churchyard.'

'I thought so, too, Patsy, but I didn't want to say anything,' said Seán.

Diarmaid and Seán Fada came to the house along with us
and drank a cup of tea.

'Great shame on ye, children, to put that much worry on
us,' said my mother. 'Dickens a notion I had that I'd ever see
ye again! I won't be in the better of it for a week, over what I
went through in the run of the night.'

I'm here today, reader, thinking about that gay, airy time
long ago. The longer a person lives the more he has to tell. It
is little thought I had then, that I'd ever be writing this story
today.

It gives delight to my heart that I had the wit to keep alive
this much of my life's story. It was often I would be listening
to rumours that there would be respect for Irish once more.
It is often too that I put questions to people over it but they
had no certainty or knowledge to give me about the story. At
that time we used to be ashamed because we didn't have any
English. But praise and thanks to the Holy Father, every life
is changing. There is respect for Irish again. It is many the
trip I made to Dingle in my young days and to tell the truth
we were little short of preferring to be dead. We were people
of no heed at all in Dingle, when we wouldn't have the English. But a big change has come over the people of Dingle
since then. The small children that are there today have
fluent Irish and so have most of the shopkeepers. It is a
grand thing that the will is coming on us to revive our language, Irish. May God and His Holy Mother grant us help
for the work.

I have this much of my life story written now. I did my
best, however, to put down a small account of my lovely sun-
village. That was the name we used to give it and we growing
up as children. I wrote this in loving memory of the place
where I was born and of the people that I knew. Some of

them are after dying, God rest their souls. Most of them are
in America, long life to them. It is a great treasure altogether
that lies hidden in a person's head. The reason for my saying
this is that, when I started on this work, I thought I wouldn't
have a half or a third as much to tell. I have finished speaking now till another day. I have a hoarse throat from talking.
God's blessing on the souls of the dead that left us and, above
all, those whose names I've mentioned in this book, and may
God grant help to those of us that are alive in this world,
until we go and visit them some fine day. I see from what's
spent of my life that a great change has come over everything
compared to when I was a gorsoon growing up. On my
solemn oath, when I think of how I spent the early part of my
life, a regret comes over me. The way I was entirely wild
about hunting! I couldn't wait for school to be over in the
afternoon, so as to call on Tom Eoin Bháin or Páidín
Mhuiris. We'd take our dogs with us and those were the dogs
that the good mettle was in them. It wasn't empty we would
come home in the evening. We'd have a fine bundle of rabbits with us. At that time, reader, I'd give the back of my
hand to any other class of sport. I was wild about it with
every bone in my body. There was no one living who would
give me an invitation for a dance or for music at that time but
I'd refuse him. I still judge hunting to be one of the best of
the sports of the Gael.

The mettle that is in a person, life wouldn't knock it out of
him. That craving is a trait in my heart today. My grief, the
last spark of that living fire that was blazing with the powerful strength of youth died out. It won't do for me to say that I
am to blame for it, that all that was hindering me was a lack
of courage. Praise for ever to the Glorious Name of the Lord,
I am not to blame, for it would suit me to be young again for
a while, but there's no way of having that, God help us. I had
my day and that's enough. If the end of my life is as hard for
me as the start was, luck won't be with me, for it was many

the bad day of rough weather and great gusts of wind and choppy seas I went through, in the course of my life. But the God of Glory and His Holy Mother brought me through it. I hope, after all the hardship, They will find room for me in the glorious kingdom, where I will be free from gloom and darkness and loneliness. But I suppose Dingle Tadgh is in a hundred places. What I'm thinking is that the likes of me is in a hundred places, praying hard to God at this present time, that He may look down on him with pity and have mercy on him.

When I think of that, it is how it sets me pondering more deeply to say that there should be anyone troubled in a place as beautiful as this world. Sure all I have to do is to look at the beautiful things God made, praise to Him for ever! Aren't they all created beautiful, as I well know, by the Holy Creator, according to His own will. As I gaze at the wonderful things, at the colours in the sky around me and the yellow golden rays of the sun coming from the West to me over the shoulder of the mountain as the evening comes on, they give peace of mind to me, although it was in loneliness I grew up, in a lonely, airy place, the Island. But I have this much to say, that there is spiritual joy to be had there for the mind in distress, on the shoulder of a mountain or beside the sea. It was often I spent a while taking my ease spread out on the brown heather, listening to the murmuring of the wind and the moaning of the waves in the coves. Reader, it is often it ran into my head to compose a piece of poetry about the thoughts that were being laid bare in my heart. But it wasn't from laziness I didn't do it, but because those pictures most pleasant to my heart were too much for me to describe.

It was a quiet and gentle life I've had of it till now. The winter itself wouldn't give me any fright, or the powerful force of the wind, or the great watery ocean itself that was a huge wall around us. It is how it used to put a glow in my heart to be looking at it and a storm there and the powerful force of a gale helping it on. It was often I spent a week in Dunquin because of bad weather, but it didn't bother me at that time; my courage was strong. I used to think it queer to see fear or dread on anyone then, like when I'd see my mother praying with all her heart to God, if it might be His own Holy Will to quieten the stretch of sea between us and Dunquin. She had her own reason for it because that was the only road the Islanders had and, to tell the truth, it is a dreadful road. I'm afraid that road won't be long there and none of the Island people will be going in and out and I suppose they won't be lonesome after it.

Maybe the best thing I could do too would be to go to sleep, for this night is cold and it is long. God bless ye, my friends, until the day brightens on us again.

SELECTIONS
FROM
COINNLE CORRA

The Great Blasket

Often with night's coming I am found
Where the sea-gull sinks in settled sleep;
The black clouds mass above me
The evening star, polished, shines bright.

On the tide's brim fish are shoaling,
Darting, skimming each current;
In midwinter the branch of evergreen
Covers the smooth hilltops of the Great Blasket.

Women and men without malice of heart
Sup satisfied in houses not rented;
The spirit of freedom is firm, untrammelled,
With young and old on the Great Blasket.

True, last night I sat down,
A full, fitting company beside me;
Our talk was the traits of our forebears,
Praising their deeds on the Great Blasket.

By all scripts of seers and druids,
The most famed in Ireland,
The tide spreads a mantle of silk
Around the Blasket Island.

A Sinner's Thoughts

A hundred thousand times I would prefer to be on that
     height west,
Tracing without fear the Sun's path;
O God, my soul would be free and safe always
Amidst the work of your hands never yet surpassed.

Stand with me, lift me again, when my strength is gone,
I am the blood-price of Him who saved the seed of Adam and
     Eve—
Black evil awaits the man who takes no thought for his last
     end,
When everyone will be swept without ceremony from the
     light of life.

Give me Your grace, O Master, and time to repent,
According to our life will death come;
So that I may spend my span piously praying;
When we lose our day, it will never return.

There is the hole where I shall lie lifeless,
Held under a heavy weight, no leave to stir—
Clay by my head, under my back, above my heart,
And the waves roaring, pounding at my feet.

O Son of Mary of Grace, Who suffered sorrowful black
     passion on the hill,
Pity my case, be gentle and answer my hoarse cry—
My soul is stained by this sin always,
Oh, do not send me for eternity to the fires of torment!

The False Voice

All are satisfied
With the false voice of the English,
Who stole every possession,
And silenced their sweet language.

They think it was not misfortune
That sent them astray—
English was their gentility,
By English they were bereft.

Ireland we do not pity,
Foreign rule hardened our hearts;
We lay down under its heel
And that heel went through us.

The Hard Crosses

How long and cold the day
In a place cheerless, unwholesome—
Sorrow! I did not spend my loan right
To gain benefit for my soul.

I made many stout attempts,
But I yielded in each heavy fight;
At the end of the hard fight
Misfortune struck again.

I would take the short cut,
Side-stepping each law,
I would be lively as a bird,
But misfortune came.

A long, fierce carrion-crow
Chased me ever, not my wish;
Peace or ease was not fated,
I had but little of it ever.

Against the shape, form, or frame
Of a power I had not known,
I was weaker than a hill-wren,
Each wound's poison poisoning me to death,

Until I fell without strength, without life,
An old man tormented by his thoughts—
Peace will be absent from me evermore,
Until I am placed amid the graveyard's bones.

I am weak today,
A poor exile by the river,
Without stock or wealth,
Sheep or horned cattle.

Waves of the receding tide,
That return again to shore—
The sense of your noise ever
Is that day does not last!

Night's Loneliness

O lovely gentle woman of the flowing curly locks,
Who changed my life and left me worthless;
Without gentle company that would tease out each knot
My life is like a bird's that has lost its nest.

It was not understanding or sense that left me unwedded to
    you,
Spending the time that is brief for everybody.
I am always alone with the thinness of night coming,
In a single bed an outcast, impotent, old.

Perversity is my lot: I come from the clay;
Falsehood, lying and the world destroying me;
The sun shines on the swan nesting—
But I am baffled why I cannot win a woman.

A Rock, Great its Fame

A rock, great its fame,
A green island in the sea,
There I first was suckled,
When I opened my eyes on the world.

It was the harsh rock,
The tide's mouth opening on it,
I knew it well,
Like all who rowed with me.

The mother who gave me life
Was the offspring of Eve's stock,
Wife of Adam, fair of shape,
That God made from the earth's clay.

We spent a while there,
In grief, sorrow, affliction,
The storm blowing daily on us,
Driving us to our downfall.

Forty years without yielding
We sheltered in our nest,
Our prop collapsed,
The trump went against us.

The light of joy did not remain,
Loneliness grew among us,
The great drive began,
That was our red shame.

Each man set off for himself,
The panic was senseless;
From that day out truly
Friend did not stand by friend.

From the day, I declare it,
When our fort of peace was destroyed,
Mist fell down on the heights,
It put us under pitiless compulsion.

This compulsion no one could fight,
Woe, how it came against us.
I wept copiously;
Each man of my friends wept.

The Door of my House was Closed

The door of my house was closed,
The reins swept from my hand.
My future is poverty,
Without court, shelter, abode.

I am in sorrow,
Coming to this cave alone—
Woeful with regret.
This place lacks all beauty.

I did not expect it,
Every voice frightens me to the heart,
Every omen is a bad omen,
My appearance shows it.

Sorrow! That height west,
Where the stream meanders on the mountain,
You are my eyes' resting place,
Yet you pierce me with affliction.

The night is long and dreary
In a lonely, black, pitiful hollow;
Sorrow! I am a prisoner here,
Looking to my freedom.

However able I am to face it,
On me hardship weighs—
Oh, if luck had been mine,
I would not be alone this night.

My fort was broken up,
Where often were pleasure and feasting.
If it had flourished,
All was well with me.

My life will be short,
Sorrow can bring you down,
I am misfortune's plaything—
Look, it abides ever.

There was compulsion on me
To settle in this glen;
My grief that I ever landed here!
A place bare and stark to my heart.

I spend a while in a trance,
Gazing at life—
I pass my days in sorrow,
It is better than to do black evil.

One Fine Morning

One fine morning and the dew heavy,
The brightness of day shining clear,
I walked on green grasslands
To breathe the moist sea air.

I sat on a sward of green grass,
I scanned every horizon;
If any man knew magic, I knew it,
With the birds' music and the Islands' scene.

The wide ocean was a lake
From the horizon to the tide's rim—
On every peak its own band,
Like a lustrous ring on a young woman's finger.

The mist streamed in ribbons of silk,
Beyond everything the fish were rising,
Shoaling on the sea's waters—
Sharp woe! Where had the boats departed?

The cormorant, black, thin-necked,
Floated like a bottle on the water,
White sea-gulls swarmed wildly,
Tearing the fish, gulping it.

There was a carpet of daisies on every side,
Growing on the green grasslands;
The scent of honey came down from the hills—
The bees were there and butterflies.

In the Lonesome Glen

Lonely I was left
Without home, fort, abode,
In a glen black, gloomy, joyless,
No noise of the gathering we knew.

I was torn from my company,
That was sweet, gay, and good once,
Each man of them clean of heart,
Standing for the rights of all.

I need to recall them
With night coming down on me—
My heart's desire to see them towards me,
I have great cause for it, and reason.

For the chattels of this life I have no desire,
To me they are not a boon;
Sorrow, I was flourishing,
Until we lost chieftain and retinue.

My Spirit will be in a Book

I am lonely in the glen,
I have only a white cat here,
But for the respect I had for my pen
I would not survive one year here.

It is no ease for a wretched man
To be in gaol, as I am—
But, however long I am prisoner here,
I shall not waste the time.

In my memories is my joy,
In my pen is my vigour,
My spirit will be in a book,
I shall live there for ever.

I shall speak to all when I am hidden away,
Like a man of the tribe everlasting;
My voice will be heard on the lips of all,
Through the lips of all I shall come.

I shall never die,
Though I shall be sent in a white shroud to the churchyard
Only my corpse will be sent there!
My voice will bloom from age to age.